GHOSTS OF GRAYHAVEN

Amy Newbold & Lark Wright

For Mom and Dad – Thanks for giving us a love of books
and reading.

CONTENTS

Chapter One

—·—

Welcome to Grayhaven

The low rumble of her motorcycle sounded like a deep-throated growl of warning as Mariah Moore approached the outskirts of Grayhaven. Rolling to a stop, she gave the black and chrome Honda café racer, the one real constant in her life, a fond pat before shutting off the engine. The two-lane highway leading into the small Oregon town was empty in both directions even though it was late afternoon. She tugged off her black helmet, tucked her blue-streaked bangs behind her right ear, and studied what she could see of the town. She'd learned from past jobs that it was always good to do a little reconnaissance before heading into unknown territory. She may never have been a boy scout, but she did believe in being prepared.

She mentally mapped what she could see of the town, noting any and all possible escape routes. Off to her left, there was an old-fashioned diner and a shabby roadside motel near the highway, with a gas station and a scattering of small houses across the street. The road curved east as it headed into town; just beyond the curve she could see what must be Grayhaven's main street. It sported a row of historic brick storefronts, two streetlights, a park across the way, and a larger building set apart from the others that might be a library, or a school. From where she sat she could also see woods, a few tree-lined streets dotted with perfect little houses, an old stone bridge, and what looked like a white steeple in the distance. The picture perfect small town.

According to her internet search, Grayhaven had been founded back in 1872 by Ezekiel Gray's family. And somehow, this nowhere town had not only survived but thrived over the past 150 years. They'd once mined stone and silver, but now Grayhaven seemed to be known for its Stone Quarry jewelry and its annual Thimbleberry Festival.

Mariah frowned. A romance writer would love this place: charming and quaint small towns seemed to be the most popular settings for those happily ever after fairy tales the Hallmark channel loved—two things she despised. She didn't do cute. And she didn't believe in cliched happy endings. Good thing she wasn't planning on being here very long. Because small town charm was not for her.

She pulled out her phone and sent off a quick text: I'm **here.**

For a moment there was no response and she was afraid it hadn't gone through. But then: **You have three days. It has to be done before the eleventh.**

Mariah rolled her eyes. Like she needed the reminder. She knew how to get a job done on time, as all her online reviews testified. **It will be,** she texted back.

This time she got no response. With a shrug she pocketed her phone, understanding instinctively that there would be no further contact until she'd finished the job.

A burst of wind ruffled her hair. It was surprisingly brisk and Mariah was grateful for her leather jacket. She'd made good time to Grayhaven, and now she would get in, do this job, and get out as quickly as possible. Though she had to admit, it was the strangest job request she'd ever gotten. She was supposed to find a specific grave and perform some weird arcane ritual. The ritual itself seemed fairly simple. Her instructions were to read some words that were either Latin or some made-up gibberish and make one tiny modification to the headstone. Okay, maybe it was more like vandalism, but the damage was so minor she figured nothing bad would happen even if she got caught. And as long as she got paid, she wasn't going to lose any sleep over it. After all, didn't rituals require belief to work? And Mariah did not believe in rituals or ghosts or anything that smacked of the paranormal. What she did believe in were her own skills to get a job like this done.

Though why anyone would pay her to do this was beyond her. But it really wasn't any of her business. That's what she loved about her kind of freelance work: no ties, no long-term commitments, and the freedom to choose where, what, and for how much. Getting involved with people and their problems just complicated life unnecessarily. And who needed that? It was better to keep things detached, anonymous even. That way there was no risk of being hurt or let down. Like with this latest job, she didn't even know if the person who'd answered her online listing was a man or a woman. And that's how she liked it. It was better not to get involved. Being shuttled from one foster home to another growing up had taught her that lesson well. Travel light and don't get attached. That was her motto. Because when you let your heart get involved, heartache always followed.

Mariah gazed off into the distance, lost in thought as she absently rubbed her thumb across the small, stylized lotus blossom tattoo on the inside of her left wrist. Lotus blossoms had to rise from the depths of murky waters in order to bloom. They were survivors. And so was she. The wind buffeted her again. With a shake of her head, she reached for her helmet. Time was wasting. Her stomach rumbled, reminding her that she hadn't eaten since early that morning. She evaluated her options. She could ride into town and look for a café, or...

She glanced across the street at the Good Eats Diner. Despite the weeds growing in the parking lot and the peeling paint that made it look abandoned, a neon sign blinked OPEN. The diner looked a little broken, as if it had seen some tough times, but it was still standing. She could respect that. Besides, diner food was the best. She'd grab a quick bite and then go look for that grave while there was still daylight. Because while Mariah didn't believe in ghosts, she also didn't relish the thought of tramping around a cemetery at night. Sometimes it was better not to tempt fate. And with that thought, Mariah headed across the street.

CHAPTER TWO

GRILLED CHEESE AND GRAVES

IT WAS THAT DEAD hour of day between the end of lunch and the beginning of the dinner rush. Zeb frowned and shook his head. Not that there was ever much of any kind of rush in the old diner these days. He glanced over at Jerry, his best regular, who was nursing his third cup of coffee and stifled a sigh, running a dishrag over the already clean Formica countertop. So this was his life now, manning his family's diner and motel, and not doing a very good job at either.

It hadn't been his plan to return to Grayhaven before he'd even finished his college degree, or to take up the family business without his dad. His funny, self-deprecating, kind and encouraging father. Growing up, it had always been just the two of them. And then he'd gotten that call from the hospital nine months ago, that unexpected, horrible phone call. Now it was just him. He reached for the silver amulet hanging around his neck, the amulet that used to be his dad's but was now his, and fisted it, his throat tight and aching. It was a reminder of the other, more important, job his father had left to him, a job at which he was also failing.

From behind, he heard a low woof and the click-clack of toenails across the floor, then felt a gentle nudge against the back of his leg. And the tight knot of sorrow around his heart loosened. He smiled and glanced down at the hound with his long black ears and dark face, intelligent brown eyes, and lean, red-boned body. "Hey, Moose, what's up?" He reached down and petted the dog's dark head, taking comfort from his presence. Moose was the best inheritance he'd gotten from his father. He'd never known a day of his life without the faithful hound always there to guide and guard him.

The bell over the door jingled and Moose disappeared into the back. Zeb looked up with a grin. "Leaving so soon, Jerry?" he called out. But it wasn't the old man shuffling out the open doorway, it was a girl coming in. And what a girl!

Zeb's cheeks flushed and an unexpected zing of attraction shot up his spine. He hadn't been interested in much lately, but she...she was interesting. She looked to be about his age, with chin-length dark hair shaved an inch above her left ear, falling longer over her right, and sporting an electric blue streak on one side. She was wearing a white tank top, green army pants and black lace-up boots, and she carried a black leather biker jacket over her left arm. Despite her slender frame, she looked tough. And way too cool for him.

He watched as her eyes took in the black-and-white photos on the walls and the faded upholstery on the booths with a look of distaste on her face, and for a moment he was sure she was going to turn around and stomp right back out. But then, with an almost imperceptible shrug of her shoulders, she marched up to the counter and sat down on one of the empty stools.

Zeb swallowed nervously and tugged at his black tee. "What can I get you?"

She studied the menu stenciled on the board behind him, then met his gaze with her own piercing stare. "What's good?" She said it like a challenge.

"Umm...people really like the chicken salad."

She frowned, unimpressed.

He tried again. "Or the BLTC is good."

"The what?"

His cheeks reddened under her intense gaze. "It's a bacon, lettuce and tomato sandwich but with an added slice of cheese...cheddar or gouda. Your choice."

She shook her head. "I don't do lettuce or tomatoes."

"I guess I could make you a bacon and cheese sandwich."

She pursed her lips, considering, then shook her head. "Make it without the bacon."

"Grilled cheese it is," he said, stepping over to the grill. "Which kind of cheese do you want?"

"Surprise me. Oh, and bring me a chocolate shake, too," she called after him.

He lifted his hand in acknowledgment, glad that her order wouldn't tax his less than stellar culinary skills. He wasn't much of a cook, which is why he let Carlos handle the dinner rush, but he could make a grilled cheese sandwich in his sleep. It didn't take him long to finish grilling the sandwich. He added some chips and a pickle to her plate before setting it in front of her. She was scrolling on her phone.

"Anything else I can get you?" he asked as he went to make her shake.

When Zeb returned with her shake, she glared at him. "Coverage here sucks."

"Internet service can be pretty spotty in town," Zeb agreed, although not for the reasons she probably thought. And once again he fingered the silver amulet around his neck.

She huffed and took another bite of her sandwich, catching the trailing cheese with the tip of her tongue. He turned away before she caught him blushing again, but he could feel the weight of her stare on his back as he pretended to swipe a spot off the counter. Steeling himself, he forced himself to turn around and meet her gaze. Her eyes were the color of sunlit amber and he forgot whatever words he'd been about to say. She surprised him by smiling.

"Maybe you can help me," she said. "I'm looking for the cemetery."

He blinked in surprise. "The cemetery?" Which cemetery did she mean? She couldn't know about the cemetery in the Hollows, could she? And his mind started racing faster than his heart. Because if she knew about that one.... He stopped the thought and forced himself to breathe. The cemetery hidden in the Hollows was warded. Protected. His family made sure of that. And no one else knew about it. He needed to relax. But he couldn't quite hide the tension in his voice. "Why the cemetery?"

"It's a hobby of mine," she said. "I like photographing old cemeteries and I hear Grayhaven has an interesting one."

He glanced away from her to hide his sudden relief. "There are some cool monuments in the oldest section. It's at the north end of town, right across from the church. You can't miss it." And he told her what road to take.

"Thanks," she said. "And thanks for the sandwich. It's good." Then she picked up her plate and shake and moved to an empty booth across the diner to finish her lunch.

He watched her surreptitiously, only looking away when he felt another nudge on the back of his legs, more insistent this time. The dog was back, hidden from view behind the countertop, looking up at him intently. Zeb peered sideways to make sure neither of his customers had noticed. Then he gave the dog's dark head a quick pat.

"That was strange, right?" he asked in a low murmur. "Her asking about the cemetery?"

The hound's intelligent gaze never wavered from his. And he felt the silver amulet warm against his chest. A warning.

Zeb nodded his head slowly, his voice dropping even lower. "I don't know what she's up to, but I think we're going to have to keep an eye on her. When she leaves, maybe you should follow her."

And Moose gave a low woof in agreement.

CHAPTER THREE

SEARCHING FOR BARTHOLOMEW KANE

THE GRAYHAVEN CEMETERY WAS tucked back at the end of a neighborhood, across the street from a quaint, steepled church. Mature trees were interspersed on the grounds, with a grove near the southwest corner. Mariah parked her motorcycle in one of the three spaces near the cemetery office. The office was closed, which was too bad for her. It would've been simpler to ask where the grave was located. Now she'd have to walk the grounds.

Mariah unzipped her jacket in the warm sunlight and set her helmet on the motorcycle seat. A crow flew overhead, its *caw caw caw* shattering the silence. It settled in a nearby tree, watching her. A breeze tugged her hair, and she reached up to tuck the blue strands behind her ear. As she headed toward the edge of the property, a second crow flapped overhead. Crows could be omens, good or bad. Mariah hoped this one was good.

Bartholomew Kane. That was the headstone she'd been hired to find. Mariah had no idea who he was, when he died, or why her client wanted her to find his final resting place, but that was all right with her. It never paid to get too invested in a job.

She started her search in the northernmost corner of the grounds. The haphazard placement of the graves was a dead giveaway that this was the oldest section of the cemetery. Headstones dotted the gentle slope. Some were tall, carved like obelisks that towered over her head. Others were rectangular slabs with a slightly curved top edge. A few of the headstones were toppled, and some were broken. She hoped the one she needed was still intact.

Mariah walked slowly, reading the names as she went. The guy in the diner was right. This part of the cemetery was quite picturesque. He'd seemed nervous when she asked about the cemetery, and she couldn't imagine why. He must have known she was from out of town, but now she wondered if he hadn't believed her when she told him she was here to take photographs. An image of his face flickered, unbidden, through her mind. He was kind of cute, but she wasn't in town to meet a guy. Mariah murmured the names on the headstones out loud to focus her attention on the task at hand.

Sarah, infant daughter of John and Matilda Gray.

Annabella Raven, beloved wife and mother.

She paused by an ornately carved stone.

Lord have mercy and keep me safe
From the evil that stalks this place.

The sentiment made her shiver. While she didn't believe the dearly departed hung around in cemeteries, someone, years ago, had clearly felt differently. She glanced around, but even the crows were momentarily silent. The cemetery was peaceful, enough, but as the sun dropped lower in the sky, she was even more eager to find Bartholomew Kane's grave before nightfall. The name on the next weathered stone was unreadable, and she traced her finger over the faint grooves to decipher the letters. While the last name seemed to be four letters long, she was confident it wasn't Kane.

She continued on and reached the end of the old section. No Bartholomew Kane. "Where are you hiding?" she said aloud.

Maybe the headstone wasn't as old as she thought. The modern portion of the cemetery was at least double the size of the old section. She surveyed the rows. Even though the stones were likely to be legible, it would take too much time to walk all of it this evening. Mariah glanced around, looking for any sign of human activity in the neighborhood surrounding the cemetery. She didn't see anyone, and hopefully that meant no one could see her.

She walked briskly over to the cemetery office and took her lock picks out of her pocket. The doorknob was a brand she'd found easy to work in the past. Mariah inserted her tension wrench and then a hook. She wiggled the hook, lifting each pin until she could turn the knob and open the door. Slipping inside, she closed the door behind her. She went first to the desk and jiggled the computer mouse. The screen remained dark. Whoever ran the office had turned the computer off when they left.

Mariah went to the file cabinet and opened the first drawer. She scanned the labels on the files, running her fingers lightly over the folders.

"Here," she said, lifting out a file with a master list of the graves. She blessed whoever had alphabetized it. Skimming down to the K section, she slowed to read each name. Not only was Bartholomew Kane not listed, but there weren't any other people on the list with Kane as a surname. Odd. He was proving annoyingly difficult to locate.

Frustrated, Mariah replaced the file and closed the cabinet. If Bartholomew Kane wasn't buried here, she needn't waste any more time at this place. Slipping outside, she locked the doorknob and pulled it closed.

The air had cooled drastically while she'd been inside. That was strange, too, on what had been a warm, summer day. As she zipped her jacket, a flash of movement caught her eye over near the grove of trees. She walked back into the cemetery to get a closer look. Elongated shadows made eerie shapes on the uneven lawn. She stopped, hands on her hips, and stared at the trees. Nothing.

"Mr. Bartholomew Kane, you are messing up my plans," she said.

A crow cawed in response. She focused on a shadowy shape with four legs and a tail. Mariah smiled in relief. This place had her on edge, but she didn't need to be nervous about a neighborhood dog. It didn't appear threatening as it watched her. The animal shifted closer to a tree, and Mariah froze. The dog was headless. She rubbed her eyes, wondering if fatigue from the long day was affecting her vision. That dog had had a head when she first saw it. She was sure of it. It had to be a trick of the light, but even as she had the thought, goosebumps rose on her arms.

The dog remained motionless. Mariah pressed her hand on her jeans to still her shaking fingers and ducked as a large, black shape flew at her. She covered her head instinctively as feathers brushed across her arm, followed by a startled squawk. She straightened and squinted at the trees, but the dog was no longer visible. Crows clustered together on a branch nearby. She counted seven of them.

Unbidden, a childhood rhyme entered her mind, and while she was fairly certain the original rhyme referenced magpies, she'd also heard it applied to crows.

One for sorrow,
Two for mirth.
Three for luck,
Four for birth.

Or in some versions, it was four for death. Which somehow was more appropriate in a cemetery.

Five for silver,

Six for gold,

Seven for a secret never to be told.

"I'd bet seven crows is a bad omen," she said. Grayhaven was certainly holding its secrets close for now, but she was up to the challenge. Mariah walked back to her motorcycle, glad to be leaving the crows behind. Cemeteries didn't bother her. She didn't believe they were haunted. But there was something unnerving about those birds. As she drove away from the cemetery, she regrouped. She had a one-night stay booked at the Grayhaven Inn just off Main Street, and in the morning, she'd find a library and do a little research on the elusive Mr. Kane.

WATCHING FROM THE SHADOWS at the edge of the cemetery, Zeb reached down and patted the silky black head of the hound standing expectantly beside him. Moose's red body quivered.

"What do you think, Moose?" he asked. "I didn't see her take any photos, and she seems pretty handy with a lock pick."

He knew Moose couldn't answer, but it was always comforting to talk to him. Especially now that Dad was gone.

"Did you hear the name she said? I wonder why she's trying to find Kane."

Zeb stared down the road where she had driven away. An outsider in Grayhaven looking for a long-forgotten grave...that set off warnings in his head. Moose whined, his sturdy tail beating against Zeb's leg.

"I don't like it, either," Zeb said. He had an unsettled feeling that he should go check on things in the Hollows. And he needed to hurry.

CHAPTER FOUR

— · —

THE SECRET CEMETERY

ZEB KNEW HE NEEDED to get to Raven's Crossing and make sure the warded graves in the small cemetery hidden deep within the Hollows were undisturbed. Especially Bartholomew Kane's. He jogged across the street to where he'd stashed his bicycle beside the church, not waiting to see if the dog followed him. Moose would find his own way there. Pedaling across town as fast as he could, Zeb turned onto an unmarked road about half a mile north of the diner. The single lane snaked through the woods, guarded on either side by tall trees, mostly rowans and alders.

Feeling a rising urgency that he couldn't quite explain, Zeb pedaled faster as he navigated the shady track that led to his childhood home. The trees and thick evening shadows lessened as he reached the wide clearing in the woods where the 110-year-old Queen Anne home stood: Raven's Crossing. It was a large, stately house. The upper windows circling the top of the round tower on the left side of the old house glinted gold in the last lingering rays of the sun, as did the second-story bay windows in front. In contrast, the deep-set front porch was sunk in shadows. Zeb could barely see the front door.

His gaze swept over the three gabled peaks of the roofline, then took in the fading gingerbread trim, the peeling paint on the dark green shutters, and the lighter green wood siding, and he sighed. The house looked bereft, almost sad. Like it knew it had been abandoned. There were no lights on, no movement, no life.

Leaving his bike in the drive, Zeb skirted around the house to the back, not ready to go inside. He hadn't been inside since his dad's funeral. It was easier living at the motel, more convenient to work and closer to town. And not so fraught with memories. But he should have been out to check on the graves in the Hollows before now. It was just...

His steps slowed as he rounded the corner of the house and saw the Raven family plot. The small patch of ground, oddly free of weeds, was set about fifty feet from the back of the house, just in front of the woods. Seven granite headstones stood like silent sentinels. One was newer than the rest. Zeb's gaze lingered on it for several long moments.

"Hey, Dad," he murmured. He started to say something else, then with a shake of his head, he hurried past the line of graves and entered the Hollows.

The light was even dimmer here, the path through the trees hard to see, but Zeb's feet easily found the way. His dad had first brought him to see the warded cemetery when he was six. Back then, those excursions through the quiet woods with his father had been another fun adventure. But now it was...different. He felt the weight of the silent trees all around him. And the shivery chill of what lay up ahead slowed his steps even more.

As he drew near the secluded graveyard, he reached for the silver amulet around his neck. He should have brought salt, rue and three white candles with him to renew the wards. Because it was overdue. But he couldn't remember all the words to the spell, and he couldn't face entering his father's study to search through all his old journals and lore books for the one with the warding spell in it.

Unshed tears burned in his eyes. He wasn't supposed to be the Keeper. Not yet. His dad was the Keeper, not him. Not this soon. He wasn't ready. He didn't even know what to do or how to do it. Hell, he didn't even know all the names on the graves in the hidden cemetery. He wished that his dad was there, that they'd had more time together. He would know what to do. But his dad was dead, and Zeb was on his own. Moose hadn't even shown up this time. Keeping this cemetery warded and the spirits inside bound was his job now. As much as he hated it, it was all on him.

Squaring his shoulders, he walked closer to the silent cemetery. An old wrought-iron fence encircled it. The pointed bars and top railing were only a few feet high, but height wasn't the point; the iron was. Zeb studied the iron gate and the graves beyond. There were eleven of them, most with raised headstones, others with flat stone markers. The weed-strewn ground around them looked undisturbed. But Zeb needed to make sure Kane's grave was still undisturbed.

Rubbing his sweaty palms on his jeans, he took a deep breath and unlatched the gate. He had to give the iron gate several hard tugs before it swung free. As he stepped carefully over the salted boundary line, the temperature around him dropped. Icy fingers crept across his skin. Zeb shivered, wishing for his jacket. And for Moose's unflappable presence. He'd never been here without the dog, or his dad. And he could feel the oppressive weight of all those damned souls buried here.

He stepped over the first grave and skirted the second, ignoring the names on these headstones. Moving cautiously, he approached the large, blackened stone at the center of the cemetery, the first grave put here. The name on it was deeply etched: Bartholomew Kane. There were runes and symbols on it, too, carved at the very top and at the two bottom corners. Zeb remembered tracing those runes with his finger when he was a boy and his father quickly pulling him back with a sharp warning. "Don't touch those!"

Back then, his father's anger had scared him more than the dark malignancy of Kane's grave, but now he could feel the cold evil buried beneath it. No wonder this cemetery always felt so frigid. What Kane had done, his dark desires and murderous depravity, permeated the air.

Out of the corner of his eye Zeb glimpsed a shadowy form rising above the iron fence. What the?! With a shout he stumbled backwards, catching his heel on the corner of a crumbling headstone and falling flat on his butt. Only then did he recognize the shadowy shape. Moose. He could barely make out the dog's black ears and head in the failing light, but it almost looked as if the hound was laughing at him.

"Very funny, Moose," he grumbled, getting to his feet.

Tail wagging, the dog trotted over to him, nimbly weaving between the stone markers, and licked his hand. Zeb pushed him away, but there was no force behind the shove. He could never be mad at Moose, and the dog knew it. Plus, he was too glad to see the red-boned hound to even pretend to scold him.

That pressing cold weight that had been bearing down on him since he'd first entered the cemetery eased. Crouching down, he studied the runes on Kane's gravestone. They looked intact as did the larger intertwined circle and triangle symbol at the top. No cracks or other marks, only soot and shadows. As far as Zeb could tell, Kane's malevolent soul remained safely bound. He breathed a sigh of relief and stood.

"What do you think, Moose? Is it all good?"

The hound uttered a low woof, but whether in agreement or not Zeb didn't know. Once again, he found himself wishing he knew what the dog was thinking. He retraced his steps across the cemetery, carefully closing and latching the iron gate behind him. Now he just had to figure out some way to keep that girl far away from here. How, exactly, he didn't know.

"Any ideas, Moose?" he asked. But when he looked down the hound was gone.

Chapter Five

Research and Psychic Nonsense

Mariah arrived at the library shortly before it opened. The red brick building had two stories. Wide steps led up to tall wooden doors, centered with perfect symmetry between four large windows. Dahlias, petunias, and verbenas bloomed in planter boxes beneath the windows. The sun was up and Grayhaven's main street was alive with people hanging Thimbleberry Festival banners on lamp posts. Mariah watched them as she waited.

Promptly at ten o'clock, an employee unlocked the doors and Mariah stepped inside. The doors opened into a wide, welcoming lobby. A couch and a few armchairs were tastefully grouped to form a reading area near a magazine rack. Mariah walked past it to the circulation desk.

"Good morning," the librarian greeted her. The woman was tall and slim. She wore a light blue blouse tucked neatly into her black trousers. Her nametag read Chloe, and her brown hair was pulled back in a messy bun. "Are you here for the festival?"

"Actually, no. I'm trying to find someone...or their headstone. Do you have any death or burial information?" Mariah asked, tucking the blue tips of her bangs behind her ear.

"Let me look," Chloe said. She typed on her keyboard and perused the computer screen. "Do you know about what year the death occurred?"

"I don't," Mariah said. She was impressed that the librarian seemed unphased by her odd request. Fielding weird questions was probably part of her job description.

"If I remember correctly, someone wrote an article last year about the cemeteries of Grayhaven. That might be helpful to you. And it looks like we have a ledger in the archives where Mabel Gray compiled a list of deaths in the area from 1872 to 1950. After 1950, I'm afraid you'd have to search the digital newspaper archive for obituaries."

She turned to Mariah. "Would you like to start with the ledger and the article?"

"That'd be great," Mariah said.

The librarian tapped more keys, and Mariah heard a printer whir to life. The woman left the desk and opened a door to a back room. Mariah glimpsed a wall of shelves, drawers, and archival boxes before the door swung closed. While she waited, she glanced around the library. A children's reading area was off to her left. To her right were taller stacks in what appeared to be the adult section. Against the far wall was a bank of computers. Other patrons walked in, settling down with newspapers or signing in for computer time.

"Here you go," the librarian said, returning to the counter. She handed Mariah a tall, thick ledger with a worn leather cover. On top of it was a printed copy of the article. "It's fifty cents for the copy."

Mariah dug through her pockets and came up with a crumpled dollar bill. The librarian handed her change, and Mariah settled in at a nearby table. She set the article aside and opened the ledger. The entries were arranged by year and written in neat, legible script. At least Mabel Gray had decent handwriting. Each entry listed the person's name, death date, and cause of death. Dropsy. Consumption. Old age. Accident at the quarry. Mariah read as quickly as possible while still being thorough. She didn't want to waste time going through this list of names again. Better to get it right the first time.

Her job often required patience. Waiting for a homeowner to leave so she could go in and retrieve a jilted lover's belongings. Waiting for the right moment to take that incriminating photo. Making sure no one was around before picking a lock. Her job consisted of doing the things people didn't want to do for themselves. She specialized in retrievals and revenge.

Mariah read the early entries in the ledger. They were sparse, and it didn't take long to cover the first few years. She guessed it was because not that many people lived in Grayhaven at its inception. She reached January 1883 and paused. A young woman had died of heart paralysis, which was odd. Mariah wondered briefly if that was an old term for a heart attack. As she continued reading, she saw the same cause of death listed four other times in the early months of the year. The entries were all for women.

She ran her finger down the list for June 1883. There it was. Bartholomew Kane.

Cause of death: shot until dead.

Not died of a gunshot wound or in a hunting accident. Shot until dead. That sounded intentional. Murder? Or something else?

Mariah pulled out her phone and took a photo of the entry. She closed the ledger and picked up the article the librarian had copied for her. The article began with a brief history of Grayhaven, information she already knew. She skipped ahead.

The Grayhaven cemetery was established in 1890, after town residents joined together to erect a church. Since 1890, Grayhaven residents have been interred in the local cemetery rather than in family cemeteries on private land.

Bartholomew Kane died in 1883, seven years before the Grayhaven Cemetery was in use. No wonder she hadn't found his headstone. Was he in a family cemetery on private land? She scanned the article to see if it listed any other cemeteries in Grayhaven. It did not. So much for a simple job.

Mariah jumped as a hand slid a paper toward her across the table.

"I drew this for you." A woman stood next to the table, her shoulder-length curly, blond hair framing a heart-shaped face and wide blue eyes. She wore a floral print dress with a wide flouncy skirt that came to her knees.

The woman gave Mariah a red lipstick smile. "Are you new here? I haven't seen you around before."

"Just passing through," Mariah said. She watched the woman's gaze travel to the death records sitting on the table.

"I'm Fleur," the woman said. "It's French for flower."

Mariah held out the drawing. "You should keep this," she said.

"Oh! No, I couldn't. I'm a psychic sketch artist, and you're meant to have that."

"Psychic sketch artist?"

Fleur laced her fingers together. "Yes! I see things about people, and I draw them."

Mariah gave the drawing a closer look. It was a sketch of a tree, showing roots and branches. There was a rectangle on the trunk of the tree with a curly-cued M in the center.

"What does it mean?"

Fleur crinkled her brow and her red lips twitched downward. "Oh, honey, I have no idea. I just draw what I see. You have to figure out the meaning."

Mariah forced a smile. She'd toss the drawing after Fleur left, but maybe Fleur knew enough about the town to be useful.

"Do you know anything about private cemeteries in Grayhaven?"

Fleur gestured to a man sitting in an armchair reading a newspaper. "Ask Jerry. If anyone knows, it's him. I've got to get to work. Have a blessed day."

As Fleur exited the library, Mariah crumpled the drawing and stuffed it in her pocket. She returned the ledger to the front desk and went over to Jerry. He didn't look up from his newspaper, and Mariah cleared her throat. Jerry peered at her over his reading glasses. His graying hair was thin on top, his face bristly with stubble. His brown eyes assessed her.

"Sorry to bother you," Mariah began, even though she wasn't sorry at all. She needed information and hoped this man could give it to her. "I'm looking for a private cemetery in Grayhaven, and I was told you're the person to talk to."

"Who wants to know? Private cemeteries are...private."

"I photograph cemeteries, and I've already been to the Grayhaven cemetery. I'm hoping to get a few more shots before I leave town."

Jerry pulled off his reading glasses and set the newspaper in his lap. "Are you from a magazine or something?"

Mariah shook her head. "I'm working on my portfolio so I have something to show potential clients. I wouldn't need to tell anyone where the cemetery is."

Jerry toyed with his reading glasses, folding and unfolding the stems. "Now why would potential clients be interested in photographs of headstones?"

The key to a good cover story was keeping it light, and not too detailed. "The subject matter is unique. It'll make my portfolio stand out from all the other landscape photographers out there."

He studied her for a moment before answering. Mariah held his gaze.

"There's one out at Raven's Crossing, the old house by the Hollows. Did you see the Good Eats Diner when you came into town?"

"Yes, I ate there," she said.

Jerry nodded in approval. "Good. Zeb needs the business. The cemetery isn't far from there. Got any paper? I'll draw you a map."

Mariah took the crumpled drawing out of her pocket and smoothed it. She handed it over to Jerry, who looked at the tree and then back at her. "What's this?"

She shrugged. "Fleur gave it to me."

Jerry tapped his finger on the M in the center. "Who's the M?"

"What do you mean?"

"The M. Whose name starts with M?"

She hadn't connected the M with anything. She figured it had to do with the type of tree. Magnolia. Maple. Why would Jerry think that the letter had something to do with her?

"Me, I guess. I'm Mariah Moore. But how would Fleur know my name?"

Jerry raised an eyebrow. "She's psychic."

Mariah didn't believe in psychics. "I'll see if there's a pen at the front desk," she said.

She returned with a pen, and Jerry sketched a map from the diner to the cemetery. Mariah was skeptical that she would find anything there in what was likely a small, family plot.

She took the map, thanked Jerry, returned the pen, and left the library.

As she got on her motorcycle, a boy who didn't look old enough to shave passed by on the sidewalk.

"Sweet ride," he said.

"Thanks."

"Honda CB350...1970?" he asked.

"You know your stuff," she replied.

He grinned, his sandy blond hair falling across his face. He tossed his hair back and stepped over to get a better view. "Chop it yourself?"

"Mostly," she said. She was pretty proud of how it turned out.

"Nice," he said, and continued on his way.

Mariah read over the information from her client on her phone. She needed some tools to fulfill this assignment.

"Hey!" she called after the boy. "Is there a hardware store nearby?"

He pointed back the way he'd come. "Go up a couple blocks and you'll see it around the corner."

She waved thanks and glanced at her phone again, making a mental list of the items she would need. If this job took much longer, it would be hard to make a decent profit. The sooner she finished it, the better. Mariah started the engine. "Hardware store, and then Raven's Crossing."

CHAPTER SIX

RAISING KANE

OF COURSE GRAYHAVEN'S ONLY hardware store would be called Nuts 'n Bolts, Mariah thought as she entered the brick-fronted store on the corner of Main and Vine. This whole town was a total Hallmark movie set, from the cutesy ice cream parlor right next door to the Tea Leaves and Good Reads bookstore across the street.

Grumbling under her breath, she moved through the store scanning the shelves as she went. She found the hammers first and chose the cheapest one; then went looking for a chisel. When she couldn't immediately find one, she grabbed a flathead screwdriver instead. It looked strong and sharp enough to chip stone.

"This should work," she said, heading down the aisle. She rounded the corner a little too fast and slammed into someone coming the other way. The hammer in her hand went flying in one direction, the screwdriver in another.

The things he'd been holding rained down onto the floor around her as she stumbled backwards.

"Watch where you're going!"

"You ran into me," the guy snapped back.

Only then did she look up, recognizing him at once as the young man from the diner yesterday. His cheeks reddened under her gaze, and he quickly looked away. He was a good head taller than her despite the fact that she was wearing her kickass black boots that gave her over an added inch in height. His brown hair, the color of café au lait, was mussed, and the front of his jeans and gray tee shirt were both dirty and damp. As he bent down to pick up the wrench, plumber's caulk, and flexible metal tubing that he'd dropped she noticed that the knuckles of his right hand were scraped and swollen. When he reached for the screwdriver and hammer, she hurried to stop him.

"I can get them."

But he beat her to it. He straightened and his eyes met hers, one a deep blue, the other a disarming hazel. It stopped her in her tracks. At the diner she hadn't bothered to really look at him, but now.... She'd never met anyone with such remarkable eyes. And the way he was studying her, so intense and serious. For a moment she couldn't look away.

He cleared his throat. "You still want these?"

She blinked and the spell cast by his unusual eyes broke. Blushing, she grabbed the two tools, muttered a quick thanks, and hurried to the front of the store to pay for them. She did not look back. A cute guy was a complication she didn't need, even one with eyes like his. Though for a brief second, part of her wished otherwise.

Outside, she shoved the tools into her saddlebags and took out the map Jerry had drawn for her, making sure she knew where she was going before climbing onto her bike. She had to backtrack twice before she found the right road. Even then she wasn't sure she was headed in the right direction, not until she reached the house. What had the old guy called it? Raven's Crossing?

She took off her helmet and slowly climbed off her bike. Raven's Crossing was the coolest house she'd ever seen. Who lived in a house like this? It was a far cry from her own cramped studio apartment. And that tower room with all those windows! What would it be like to spend the night up there stargazing? It was like something out of a fairy tale. Which made her scowl. Fairy tales weren't real; she'd learned that long ago.

Grabbing the tools and her phone, she stomped past the front walk and followed the wraparound porch to the back of the house. The wide lawn was a tangle of clover, morning glory and unmowed grass. It was bordered on all three sides by deep woods. She paused and scanned the yard. It was empty. And silent. No birds singing, no insects buzzing. At the far end stood seven headstones. Her heart beat faster. Was it the cemetery she was looking for?

Throwing a quick glance over her shoulder to make sure no one was watching her from any of the house's many windows, she quickly crossed the yard to the first headstone. She read the name on it, then moved on down the row: Mathias Raven, Thomas Mathias Raven, Benjamin Raven, Jebediah Raven, Nathaniel J. Raven, Zebulon Thomas Raven, and Thomas Benjamin Raven. The dates of their deaths ranged from 1907 to just last year. So many Ravens! Must be where the house got its name. She looked back at it once more, but all the windows and doors remained shut and dark. It didn't look like anyone was home. Or if they were, they were staying hidden. She circled the raised stone markers once more, but there were no other visible names. She frowned. These seven graves couldn't be the old cemetery Jerry meant. Where were the women? And children? More importantly, where was Bartholomew Kane? With her hands on her hips, Mariah scanned the entire yard, then moved back to study the surrounding woods.

"Come on," she muttered. "It's got to be here somewhere."

Her eyes caught on a darker line of shadow threading through the trees, and an icy breath of air snaked down her spine. What was that? She took a careful step closer to the trees, then another. Was that...?

A path! She raised her arms about her head in triumph. And without stopping to question the feeling in her gut that told her this was what she'd been looking for, she started off down the shaded track through the woods at a jog. She kept her eyes peeled for rocks and roots as her boots thudded dully against the hard-packed dirt. A breeze set the leaves on the trees trembling; it seemed to whisper in her ears. Was it telling her to hurry, or turn around and go back? She wasn't sure. Then, up ahead in a ragged clearing of trees, she saw it.

This cemetery wasn't very big, but the thick silence enshrouding it was eerie. Mariah moved closer and eyed the low iron fence encircling the graves. All the headstones within looked old and worn, but there weren't very many of them. Why were they so close together? And why was this cemetery even out here in the middle of these woods? There was something strange about this place.

Ignoring her unease, Mariah hopped the iron fence. A thousand needle-sharp pinpricks ghosted across her skin. Then it was gone. She frowned, rubbing her arms against the sudden chill that followed. She didn't like this place. The sooner she got this job done the better. She scanned the names on the nearest gravestones. Bradshaw. Ransom. Gray. And then, on the oddly blackened headstone standing in the center of the cemetery she saw it. Bartholomew Kane.

Kneeling in front of the stone, Mariah studied the indecipherable runes carved into the bottom two corners of the stone and wondered what they meant. She'd never seen anything like them. She pulled out her phone. Whoever had hired her had sent her pictures of the two runes she was looking for; she had to trace each one as she said some crazy Latin words. At least she thought it was Latin. But who really knew? It's not like she'd studied it at school.

She matched the first rune on her phone to the middle rune in the bottom righthand corner of the headstone. Drawing in a deep breath, she carefully traced the downward middle stroke and the three crossed lines.

"Confractus."

The stone felt oily beneath her fingers, and she fought the urge to scrub her whole hand clean on her pants. The next rune was in the bottom lefthand corner. She traced the two zig-zag lines and spoke the next word.

"Exsolvo."

Now for the tricky part. Mariah quickly glanced around the clearing to make sure no one was watching her. Then she put the tip of the screwdriver against the raised stone circle surrounding an upside-down triangle at the very top of the headstone and took a tight grip on the hammer. She just had to chip away enough of the stone to break the circle. How hard could it be?

She hit the end of the screwdriver with her hammer. The metal edge skidded off the side of the circle leaving a long scratch on the face of the stone. Mariah swore under her breath. Repositioning the screwdriver, she hit it even harder. Once again it slipped off before doing any damage to the raised circle. Mariah eyed it darkly. Maybe she should have looked harder for a stone chisel at the hardware store. She shook out her hand holding the hammer. Or maybe...

She gripped the hammer with both hands, took aim, and swung it hard at the top edge of the circle. The resulting ring hurt her ears and stung her palms, but she'd managed to make a small crack in the stone. Another hit or two should do it.

The low baying of a hound echoed through the woods. Mariah glanced behind her but didn't see anything. The baying sounded again, closer. And this time she heard a man's shout along with it. Knowing she had to hurry, Mariah quickly read out the rest of the spell in a loud voice.

"Vincula solvere. Constitui te liberatus!" And she swung the hammer hard at the top of the circle. The crack fissured.

"No!"

Two figures burst from the woods, the young man from the hardware store and a large, red-boned hound. They raced toward her. Mariah swung the hammer one last time. She caught the top of the stone circle in just the right spot. There was a loud crack, and the top of the circle broke completely off. She'd done it.

For a moment the air seemed to freeze. Then a deep thrumming reverberation rose up from the ground. It rumbled like thunder. A sudden shock of energy surged through her body, knocking her backwards. She fell to the ground. Then all went quiet except for the unnatural ringing in her ears and the low menacing growl of the dog.

Chapter Seven

Moore Mayhem

Moose bounded over to the girl lying beside the headstone. The hound positioned himself between her and Kane's grave, dark head lowered, hackles raised. Zeb rushed after the dog, storming inside the cemetery. In horror, his gaze darted between Moose, the cracked head-stone, and the girl on the ground.

A gust of wind buffeted his back and the silver amulet around his neck began to burn like cold fire. Something was very wrong. He half-turned. Moose uttered a loud bark, and Zeb felt the dog's paws thump against his back, then the dog's heavy body knocked him to the ground. A rush and roar of unseen power blew over him. Dirt, twigs, and small rocks pelted his body. Zeb covered his head. Moose barked twice more. The cemetery fell quiet.

Zeb lifted his head. He glanced over at Moose, then at the girl. They looked unharmed. He slowly got to his feet and dusted himself off. Whatever had attacked him was gone. And so was the unbound soul of Bartholomew Kane. He glared at the girl responsible.

As the shadow dissipated, anger replaced the fear inside Zeb. The girl stirred, and she pressed her hand to her forehead with a groan.

"What have you done?" he shouted at her, his voice hoarse with rage.

She scooted backwards, pale and obviously shaken, but Zeb was too angry to care about that.

"Who the hell are you anyway?" he asked.

"None of your business," she said, her voice trembling. Her gaze slid to the hammer lying on the ground next to the cracked headstone and her face flushed. "I was just doing a job."

Zeb's eyes widened in disbelief. "A job? Do you know what kind of evil you unleashed?"

"I cracked an old headstone. It's no big deal."

He grabbed her arm as she scrambled to her feet. "You broke more than a headstone. If we don't figure out how to replace those wards, there's no telling what Kane will do, or how many people could get hurt."

Her eyes blazed with anger as she yanked her arm free of his grasp. "That's not my problem."

Before he could say anything else she stomped away, hopping over the cemetery fence and disappearing into the woods. Zeb's shoulders sagged.

She was right. It wasn't her problem. It was his.

He didn't have the first clue how to begin to put it right. But he did have an idea where to go to look for some answers. Still, his feet didn't seem to want to move. Because the mere idea of having to enter his father's study and go through his books and papers made his stomach hurt.

If only he'd spent more time with Dad when he had the chance. When Dad wanted him to help set the wards, Zeb had been too busy. He figured he would always have time to learn, that his Dad still had years ahead to teach him.

He reached for the amulet hanging around his neck. It no longer burned to the touch, but it felt heavy in his hand. His father would be so disappointed in him. and that was almost more than he could bear.

At his side, Moose nudged his leg. Zeb glanced down at the hound's dark face, his heart aching. "I didn't protect the wards," he said. "And I have no idea what to do now, or how to put them back."

Moose licked his fingers in response. Then the dog jumped over the cemetery fence and headed for the path. At the edge of the woods, he paused to look back at Zeb. Then he barked once. It was clear what he wanted. Zeb took one last look at Kane's damaged headstone. He couldn't do anything about it right now. Making his way out of the cemetery, he followed the red-boned hound through the woods back to Raven's Crossing.

The silence in the house was oppressive as Zeb walked inside. The musty smell made it hard to breathe, and a thick layer of dust covered every surface. He felt another wrench of guilt at the sight; he should have come sooner. Bypassing the kitchen and living room, he headed for the stairs. He passed his bedroom and paused momentarily in front of the closed door to his dad's bedroom. He continued on down the dark hall to the narrow staircase that led to the tower room. Zeb climbed the steps with heavy feet. At the door to his father's study, he looked back for Moose, but the hound had stayed downstairs. Taking a deep breath, he pushed the door open and stepped inside.

His dad's messy desk dominated the room. It was just as he'd left it, with an unfinished crossword puzzle in the middle, a scattering of books and bills, and the miscellaneous papers he'd been working on before his death. There was a curved window seat that ran below the four tall windows spaced along the outer wall. That was where Zeb had sat for hours as a kid, reading and dreaming while his dad worked on his research. You could see for miles out those windows. Behind his father's desk, on the other side of the door, was the large built-in bookcase. It was crammed with well-read paperback novels, history books, books in ancient Greek and Latin, esoteric spell books and arcane treatises on ancient languages and symbols. It also held all the leatherbound journals from each past Keeper.

Zeb knew he should probably start with those first. They should have some information about Kane and the cemetery wards. But he went and sat down at his dad's desk instead. He brushed his fingers across the folded New York Times crossword puzzle that his father had always done in pen. If only his dad were here now; he'd know what to do. Zeb opened one of the desk drawers, found only a mess of paper clips, pens and Post-it notes, then opened another one.

His breath caught in his throat when he saw an envelope with his name on it. Had his father left him instructions? But when he opened it, he saw only a handful of photographs. He thumbed through them one by one. They were all of him and his dad: the two of them fishing together at the river, his dad teaching him to ride his first bike, one of them at his tenth birthday party. Camping. His high school graduation. The day he left for college. It was hard to swallow around the lump in his throat, and tears burned his eyes.

He grabbed all the photos and put them back in the envelope. Then he picked up one of his dad's many bookbags and stuffed the first leatherbound journal into it. A slim volume toppled out of the bookcase and fell onto the floor; Zeb threw it into the bag. He scanned the titles of spell books and found one that seemed to be about wards and amulets, and he crammed that one in the bag, too. Last, he found his dad's own Keeper journal. Taking the envelope of photos and the bag of books, he headed for the stairs.

Moose met him at the front door, blocking his way. The red-boned hound gazed up at him with those dark knowing eyes. Zeb shook his head.

"I can't right now, Moose," he said. "I need to get back to the motel and finish fixing that leaky connection, and then I should check on Carlos at the diner, and return his truck to him..."

Moose didn't move. They were feeble excuses and both he and the dog knew it.

Zeb slumped against the doorframe, exhausted and overwhelmed. "I can't be here right now, Moose," he whispered. "It's too hard."

With a low whine, Moose shifted out of the way and followed Zeb to the truck. Zeb opened the door and Moose hopped inside. Once Zeb was settled, the hound laid his head on Zeb's leg. The dog's warmth was comforting as they drove back to the diner. Zeb left the truck for Carlos and headed to the motel office. Moose stayed close by, and Zeb wasn't sure if the dog was there to protect him, or to remind him that he had other, more important things that he needed to do. Either way, he was grateful for the dog's company.

"Hey, Moose," he said. "Want to lock up and go get some tacos and ice cream?"

The dog's tail thumped happily against the floor in response.

CHAPTER EIGHT

GHOSTED

MARIAH DROVE HER MOTORCYCLE as fast as she dared, eager to get out of Grayhaven. As soon as she was safely out of town, she'd stop and text her client.

"Almost there," she said as she passed the Good Eats Diner. She shivered, still feeling a chill from the cemetery. She refused to believe anything supernatural had come out of the grave when she'd damaged the headstone.

To her relief, when she glanced over her shoulder no one was following her. And there wasn't a cop in sight, either. A few more yards and she'd be outside of the city limits. But as she neared the edge of town, her motorcycle made a belching noise and sputtered to a stop. She turned the key, but the engine didn't start.

"You have got to be kidding me," she muttered, pushing the bike to the side of the road. She tinkered around for a moment but couldn't find anything wrong. Her gas tank was nearly full, and there was no visible reason for the machine to quit working like that. With a sigh, she pushed it back up the road a few yards and tried the engine again. This time, it started with no problem. It had to have been a fluke.

But when she reached the spot where the motor had died moments ago, it happened again. She backed the machine up, but this time it didn't start. Her frustration mounted, and she was suddenly very tired. All she wanted was a hot shower and a clean bed.

It was dark, and she didn't relish the thought of waiting by the side of the road in hopes of some sort of rescue. There was a motel by the diner, not too far from where she was. Maybe she could stay there tonight and figure it all out in the morning. With a sigh, she pushed her bike across the street and headed back toward town.

She'd worked up a sweat by the time she reached the motel. The sign identified it as the Welcome Inn, but it didn't look very welcoming, and it was certainly not an inn. It was one of those rundown motels she'd often seen in small towns, the kind where the building was one row of rooms, doors all facing the parking lot. To her surprise, there were several cars parked outside. She left the bike in an empty space and headed for the motel office, grateful to see the flashing *Vacancy* sign.

She entered the room and stopped cold because the guy behind the counter was the guy she'd just left in the cemetery. The same guy she'd seen in the hardware store. And at the diner. It was like fate was throwing them together. And fate had a sick sense of humor. He was the last guy she wanted to see right now, and by the expression on his face, a mixture of hate and loathing, he must feel the same way about her.

"You have a lot of nerve showing up here," he said, glaring at her. "You need to leave. Now."

So much for the Welcome Inn sign. It was apparent she wasn't welcome here at all. This day couldn't possibly get any worse. If her motorcycle hadn't stopped at the edge of town, she'd be long gone by now, but without transportation, she was stuck.

Mariah lifted her chin and squared her shoulders. Confidence. No apologies. Least said soonest mended.

"I need...my bike...I couldn't leave...place to sleep," she said. Her voice cracked, and her words were garbled. This wasn't like her at all. She sounded like an idiot.

He stared at her for a long moment, and she considered leaving. But where would she stay tonight? She was much too tired to push her bike all the way into town, and she was not about to sleep by the side of the road. She tried again.

"Look, I just really need a room."

He studied her for a moment and glanced over her shoulder out into the parking lot. "I forgot to change the sign. Sorry." He crossed his arms, his face grim.

"Please. I don't have anywhere else to go." Mariah hated the pleading tone in her voice, but she would do what was necessary.

"Not my problem," he said.

As tired as she was, she admired the way he threw her words back at her. She pulled out a wad of bills from her jacket pocket. "I have cash."

She heard a rattling noise behind the counter, followed by a whine. To her surprise, the dog from the cemetery was nudging the man, a key dangling from his mouth. Not a card like most of the places she'd stayed, but an old-fashioned key on a fob with a room number on it.

"No, Moose. She can't have a room, not after what she did." He took the key from the dog and tucked it into a drawer.

The dog glanced at her and back at the guy. He disappeared behind the counter, and she heard the same rattling noise as before. When the dog reappeared, he had another key in his mouth. This time, tail wagging, he circumvented the guy and brought the key directly to her. The dog was even larger up close in this small space than he'd seemed in the cemetery. She took the key, ignoring the fact that it was wet with drool.

The dog sat and she could've sworn he was grinning at her. His tail thumped twice on the floor. He'd let her know who was in charge here. Come to think of it, he'd let the guy behind the counter know who was in charge, too. The dog's black head contrasted with his rust-colored body, and she wondered what breed he was.

With a sigh, the man tapped on the computer screen. "I need I.D. and a credit card."

"I'm paying with cash," she protested.

"No card, no room. I need it on file in case you *damage* anything else."

Mariah hesitated. It had been a mistake to tell that guy, Jerry, her name. She didn't need it on record somewhere else in town. Staying anonymous kept her out of trouble more often than not.

The door chimed, and a woman walked inside, looking frazzled. She stood behind Mariah, so close that Mariah wanted to explain to her about personal space.

The guy nodded to the new customer and turned his attention back to Mariah. "Look, if you don't want the room, I need you to step aside."

"If she doesn't want the room, I'll take it," the woman said. "Every place in town is full because of the Festival."

"I'll take it," Mariah said, setting her driver's license and credit card on the counter.

He picked up her cards. "Mariah Moore?"

"That's me."

He frowned as he processed her information, his silence pressing against her. If that woman hadn't been standing there, she'd have asked him what the energy was that knocked her flat in the cemetery. Maybe. She could tell he didn't want to talk to her. She thought about asking him if he knew a good mechanic and decided she could wait. She'd take a look at the bike in the morning and see what she could figure out.

"That'll be one hundred and seventy-five dollars."

She started to protest the rate, but clamped her mouth shut as she counted out the bills and slid the cash across the counter.

"You're in room five," he said, picking up the money.

Mariah held up the numbered key. "I kind of guessed." She picked up her driver's license and card and tucked them back in her phone case. "Wi-Fi password?"

He frowned at her, his eyes stormy. Those mismatched eyes. She tried to ignore the fluttery feeling they gave her.

"Never mind," she muttered and scurried out the door.

Once outside, Mariah inhaled to clear her head. She grabbed her saddlebags off her bike and headed to room five. The key stuck in the door, and she had to wiggle it to get it to turn, but eventually it opened, and she stepped warily inside the room.

Despite the outward appearance of the motel, the room interior was neat and clean. The carpet was a bit worn, but the walls looked like they'd been painted recently. She dropped her saddle bags on the floor. The air was stuffy, and she turned the knob on the air conditioning unit. It roared to life, the fan vibrating with a steady noise. First order of business, text her client.

She pulled out her phone. It was dead, which was odd, since it had been fully charged before she went to the cemetery. The lamp had a charging port, and she plugged it in and settled on the lone chair in the room.

It's done.

Three dots appeared beneath her text, and she waited for a response. But the dots disappeared. Mariah continued to watch the screen. She was hungry and tired, and she wanted to finalize this job and move on.

You can send payment now, as we agreed.

Her phone buzzed. The text wasn't delivered. She sent it again.

Undelivered.

She opened her payment app, but no payments had been sent. Damn. Anger pulsed inside her as her head began to throb. She'd come all this way, and done the job, and now she was being ghosted? She'd been stiffed on a job before, but not for a long time.

She tried calling the number. Maybe it was time she spoke with her client. It might be harder for them to put her off on an actual call.

A mechanical voice informed her the number she had reached was no longer in service. How was that even possible? Her text had gone through moments ago.

She set the phone down and slapped the top of the table in frustration. She had no way of tracking down her client.

"Stupid, stupid, stupid." Mariah leaned forward, elbows on her knees, and cradled her face in her hands. Grayhaven was no haven for her.

A MAN WAS FOLLOWING her. Mariah hurried down the street, trying to shake him, but every time she turned around, he was there.

His face was thin and angry, his eyes shadowed by a hat pulled low over his forehead. Cold swept right through her and she shivered, unable to move, unable to run away. Ever so slowly, the man's mouth opened into a menacing grin. His fury was palpable and directed at her. He moved closer, and his hot breath raked over her skin.

She shrieked and jerked awake, her heart pounding. She was completely disoriented, and it took her a moment to remember where she was. Her eyes gradually focused in the dim light. She picked up her phone and checked the time. 2 AM. The room was chilly, and she shivered as she got up to change the temperature on the air conditioning unit. Her hand shook as she turned the knob.

She peered out the window, trying to shake off the remnants of the dream. The big hound dog lay outside her door, and she found his presence strangely reassuring. While she watched, he lay his head down on his paws and appeared to sleep. She returned to bed, wrapping herself in the covers until she stopped shivering and finally drifted back to sleep.

G RAYHAVEN LIVED UP TO its name this morning, bland and gray as the day dawned. Her neck ached, and so did her back. It was a painful reminder of her fall at the cemetery when she'd been knocked over by some unseen force yesterday. Mariah rummaged in her saddlebags for some pain reliever and went into the bathroom for a cup of water to wash the pills down.

Her hair was sticking up at unruly angles and she had dark circles under her eyes. She picked up a cup and turned on the tap. When she glanced in the mirror, an unfamiliar face was staring back at her. She dropped the cup and water splashed on her bare feet. She spun around, but no one was behind her. Turning back to the mirror, she saw a young woman gazing at her. She wore a white, high-necked blouse, her hair braided and coiled around her head. Mariah gripped the counter. This wasn't real. This couldn't be happening.

As quickly as the image appeared, it was gone. This place had gotten in her head. Mariah clung to the counter, willing her heartbeat to return to a normal rhythm. She didn't believe in ghosts. It was simply a trick of her tired mind. When her hands steadied, Mariah picked up the cup, refilled it, and swallowed the pain reliever.

"The sooner I get out of this place, the better," she muttered.

She left the bathroom and got dressed. As she packed her few belongings in the saddle bags, she saw a paper slide under the door.

She walked over and picked it up, expecting an invoice for her stay. Instead, it was a drawing. And not a very good one. A curly-cued M was on the paper, and a picture of a guy, one of his eyes darker than the other one. "Talk to Zeb" was written on the paper in block letters. It had to be from that psychic lady, Fleur.

Now Mariah was annoyed. She didn't appreciate Fleur stalking her to the motel and giving her this. Something was very wrong with the people in this town.

She studied the drawing and had to admit there was a resemblance to the guy at the diner. More of a likeness than just his mismatched eyes. Jerry told her Zeb needed the business when she said she'd eaten there. Now she knew his name, but there was no way she was going to talk to him. She'd had enough of Grayhaven and everyone in it.

Chapter Nine

Trouble at the Thimbleberry Festival

The morning seemed to be holding its breath as Mariah snuck out of her room. She crossed the parking lot quickly, not wanting the motel guy to spot her leaving and demand her room key back. Because she might still need it. Especially if she couldn't get her motorcycle working before night.

Circling her bike, she wiped a smudge from the chrome and patted the black leather seat. "Feeling better?" She didn't have much hope that it had somehow magically fixed itself overnight, but still she got on and tried to start it. When the engine revved to life, she nearly fell off in surprise. Revving the engine again, she grinned. "You're the best."

Now she could get the hell out of Grayhaven and forget about everything that had happened here. Though she was still pissed about not getting paid. But finding out who hired her and tracking down the money she was owed was a fight for another day. She tugged on her helmet and headed for the highway. Less than one mile down the road, the engine sputtered and died, just like it had done yesterday. She rolled to a stop. Swearing under her breath, she tried everything she could think of to get it started again. Nothing worked. It was like something didn't want her to leave town.

A truck rumbled up behind her. She turned and saw the old man from the library rolling down his window. "Need some help, Missy?"

"Is there a bike shop in town?" she asked.

Jerry scratched his forehead. "Abe's Auto Shop is probably your best bet," he said. "I can give you a lift into town if you want, though I doubt they're open yet."

"That's okay," Mariah said, eyeing her bike. She'd pushed it before, she could do it again.

"It's no trouble," Jerry insisted, stepping out of his truck. "I'm heading in that direction anyway for the annual Thimbleberry Pancake Breakfast. They serve the best pancakes around, and I always buy the first stack." He checked his watch, then walked around to the back of his truck to lower the tailgate. He heaved out an old board to use as a makeshift ramp. "So we'd best get 'er loaded up if you want a ride."

Mariah helped load her motorcycle into the bed of his truck, then climbed into the passenger seat. "Thanks for this."

Jerry waved it off. "Not a problem," he said, putting his truck into gear and heading down the road. "Silver lining? It'll give you a chance to try some of those pancakes while Abe works on your bike."

As they passed the motel and diner, Jerry shot her a quick sideways glance. "Did you ever find that cemetery I told you about?"

For a moment Mariah thought about telling him the truth, then shook her head. "No."

Jerry pursed his lips. "It's probably for the best. Zeb wasn't too happy when I told him I'd sent you out there."

Zeb. The name on the note. She discreetly checked her front pocket to make sure it was still there. Not that she knew what to do with it. This town! A true silver lining for her this morning would have been a motorcycle that worked, the money she was owed in her account, and a new, more normal, job on the horizon. Instead, she was stuck in Grayhaven for who knows how long.

They dropped her bike off at Abe's, then Jerry took her to the Main Street Plaza in the center of town where he left her to go claim his stack of pancakes. The square was arrayed with berry-colored banners hanging from every lamppost and booths lining the sidewalks for the Thimbleberry Festival. They'd even set up a small stage on the south end of the plaza, but it was empty as were most of the booths. Apparently, the Festival didn't officially get going until noon. But when it did it looked like there would be everything from Thimbleberry scones and syrup for sale, to tee shirts, candles, and Stone Quarry jewelry. There was even a booth sign that read: Tea Leaves and Tarot readings.

Despite the festive air, Mariah felt uneasy. Maybe it was just the aftereffects of her unsettling dream last night, or that ghostlike figure she'd glimpsed in the mirror. But Grayhaven felt less like a Hallmark movie set this morning and more like the opening scene of a horror movie.

A black crow flapped overhead, cawing. Mariah watched it land on top of the life-sized bronze statue in the middle of the plaza. The bird eyed her curiously as she walked closer. One crow for sorrow. It sat for a moment atop the statue, then flew off. Mariah read the plaque at the bottom: Ezekial Gray, founder of Grayhaven. The man's bearded face was stoic, his mouth unsmiling. She gazed up at him a moment, then wandered over to the front of the stage. There was a board off to the side listing the musical groups that would be playing there throughout the afternoon and evening. An unnerving breeze tickled the back of her neck as she read the schedule. Overhead, a second crow cawed a warning. Then a strong gust of wind buffeted her back and she heard a loud screech of metal.

"Watch out!"

A strong hand yanked her backwards as a metal bar with spotlights attached to it crashed to the ground right where she'd been standing. Her feet tangled with her rescuer's as she stumbled backwards, and they fell to the ground. She pushed herself up to a sitting position and looked over at him. It was him, the guy from the cemetery, and his dog. Again.

"Are you all right?" he asked.

The wind kicked up into an angry roar before she could answer. It whipped around the plaza, tearing down banners, knocking over signs, and rattling booths. Mariah scooted backwards toward the center of the square, dodging the falling debris. The guy scrambled to his feet as the large dog started to bark. Behind her, the bronze statue began to sway back and forth. Then, with a loud groan, it toppled over, smashing to the ground right next to her. She yelped and rolled away. The angry gust roared over her head. Then it was gone.

She sat up, heart beating fast, and looked wildly around the plaza, waiting for the next thing to careen her way. Instead, the square fell eerily silent. The guy glanced down at the dark-headed hound. "See if you can track him down, Moose." Then he came over to her and held out his hand. She let him help her to her feet. "You okay?"

She gazed up at him warily. He looked tired and weighed down with worry, and she had a sneaking suspicion it was all because of her. She just didn't know what to do about it.

The large hound brushed past her. She watched him trot across the plaza. As he passed a row of booths it looked for a moment like his head disappeared, just like that shadowy dog she'd seen at the town cemetery.

Several townspeople came running onto the plaza, exclaiming when they saw the damage the wind had done. Mariah glanced over at the guy. He was watching her with an angry frown. Not that she blamed him. She swallowed hard and took a chance. Digging into her pocket for the sketch she'd found under her motel door earlier that morning, she held it out to him. "Are you Zeb?"

He seemed reluctant but resigned as he took the paper from her and unfolded it. He stared down at the sketch of his face and Fleur's message. Then his mismatched eyes met hers.

"Looks like we need to talk," he said, folding up the sketch and handing it back to her. He ran a hand through his mussed hair and offered her a rueful smile. "But for this conversation, I'm going to need some pancakes." His disarming eyes took in the wreckage around them, and he amended his words. "A **lot** of pancakes."

CHAPTER TEN

DEAD RECKONINGS

THE MAYOR WALKED TO the center of the plaza, a bright smile on her face. "Looks like we have a windy welcome this morning, folks! I encourage you to come get a pancake breakfast while our vendors get their booths put back together."

The smell of pancakes filled the air. Zeb nodded in the direction of the food line, and Mariah followed him as he made his way through the debris.

"Thanks for saving me," she said.

Zeb grunted. He was still mad at her about Kane. He rolled a plastic knife and fork in a napkin and stuffed it in the pocket of his jeans, leaving his hands free to carry his plate and drink. He stopped at a table to butter his pancakes. Mariah drowned hers in thimbleberry syrup. He watched the thick, red liquid spill over the edge of her pancakes, surrounding them in a lake of syrup.

"You're going to need more pancakes to mop that up," Zeb said.

She smiled, and despite everything, despite the trouble that followed her like a tornado, he liked the way her smile lit up her whole face.

"I don't want to ruin perfectly good syrup with a bad pancake ratio," she said.

The corners of his mouth twitched upward, weakening his determination to stay mad at her. Zeb chose a table far from the other early-breakfast eaters. Mariah settled into the seat across from him. Maybe she really didn't have any idea what would happen when she bashed Kane's headstone.

"I thought you'd be long gone," Zeb said.

She swallowed a mouthful of syrup-soaked pancakes. "And miss all this?" The smile left her face and she sobered. "I would be gone but my bike broke down. Again."

Zeb put his fork down. "Where?"

She shrugged. "Not far from the motel as I was leaving town."

"You know what all this is, don't you?" he asked, gesturing toward the plaza. "The wind, the statue, your bike, it's all because of you. What you did. Why would you release Bartholomew Kane?" He kept his voice low, not wanting the people milling around the plaza to hear him.

"It was a job," she said, fingering her napkin. "What does it matter to you?"

"That was my property you were trespassing on and…"

Moose appeared next to Zeb, his intelligent eyes looking hopeful. Zeb picked up half a pancake and held it out. Moose gulped it down and thumped his tail, asking for more. Zeb tried to ignore the dog. His body was still wound tight as a coiled spring. Zeb swallowed a bite of breakfast with difficulty and took a drink to wash everything down. Moose laid his head on Zeb's thigh.

"My client hired me to perform a ritual at a grave and that's what I did," Mariah said.

"And you didn't think about what could happen?"

She shook her head. "I didn't think anything *would* happen. Who believes that stuff?"

Zeb flinched. He believed. His whole family did. The pre-mature death dates on the Raven headstones on his property were proof enough that some things were real and best kept hidden.

Moose put his paws on the table and nuzzled Zeb's cheek. Zeb rubbed the sides of the dog's face.

"You just want my pancakes." Moose licked his face.

"What's his name?" Mariah asked.

"Bottomless pit," Zeb said. Moose sat down and put his paw on Zeb's knee. "I call him Moose. His real name is Zigmund, but I couldn't say it when I was little."

"Zigmund?"

"It means victorious protector," Zeb said.

"How long have you had him?"

Zeb fed Moose another piece of pancake. "He's been in my family forever. He belonged to my dad, and now he's mine. Like the cemetery."

Mariah frowned. "Dogs don't live that long. And what's up with that cemetery, anyway?"

Zeb shook his head. It was impossible to explain. Moose was simply...Moose. And as for the cemetery, he barely understood it himself. "That cemetery protected all of us from the people locked away in it. Until you broke it."

Mariah soaked her last piece of pancake in syrup and put it in her mouth. A red, sticky drip ran down her chin. She swiped at it with her napkin.

"I'm sorry something bad is loose in town. But I think Grayhaven is going to survive a little wind."

"But will you?" Zeb asked. "It was targeting you. And it's not just wind. Why do you think you couldn't leave town?"

"You think Kane is targeting me? Why?" she asked.

Zeb shrugged. "I don't know, but he's angry. I can feel that."

He rose to his feet, letting Moose take the last pancake from his plate. He needed to put Bartholomew Kane back in that grave as soon as possible, and that meant he needed to get home. Not the motel, but Raven's Crossing. If Kane had been locked in that cemetery once, it could be done again. He hoped.

As they walked by the toppled statue, Mariah pointed to the plaque. "Ezekiel Gray. Why would Kane knock over his statue?"

"Good question," Zeb said. "Maybe they had history together."

Zeb wasn't interested in researching town history. His task was to figure out how to restore the wards and lock Kane away. It was a big enough task, one that filled him with uncertainty and dread.

Mariah looked like she wanted to say something else, but an ear-splitting siren filled the air. She covered her ears. "What is that?"

"Fire alarm," Zeb said, as volunteers scrambled to their feet. Grayhaven was a quiet place, and he could count on one hand the number of times the fire department had been called into action in the last year. Was this because of Kane, too?

"Come on," he said to Mariah, grasping her hand and breaking into a run. When he reached the fire station, he grabbed the first person he recognized.

What's happening?" he asked.

The man set down a pair of boots and clasped Zeb on the shoulder. "There's a fire...at Raven's Crossing."

Chapter Eleven

Fire at Raven's Crossing

Raven's Crossing was not engulfed in flames...yet. But there was a lot of smoke, mostly coming from the tower room's four broken windows. It looked like that's where the fire had started. The volunteer firefighters were already working to put it out.

Mariah glanced at Zeb and tried to summon an encouraging smile. "At least the fire department got here fast."

Grim-faced, Zeb kept his gaze on the tower. His hands were clenched into two tight fists and it looked like he was ready to storm the house. Oh how she knew that feeling of helplessness and anger. As a foster kid growing up, she also knew how it felt to lose everything that matters without any warning. It made her stomach hurt just thinking about it.

"Zeb?" She softly touched his arm. "It's going to be okay."

He jerked away from her, anger blazing in his eyes. "It's not okay. Everything I need to stop Kane is in that room! Without it..." His voice trailed off. Grief washed over his face, and for a moment he looked so lost and alone Mariah couldn't help but step closer. He barely spared her a glance. "I've got to get in there!"

Before she could stop him, he strode determinedly toward the house. A fireman quickly blocked his path. Mariah couldn't hear what the man said, but after a moment Zeb took a reluctant step back. But his gaze remained fixed on the tower.

Wishing she knew what to say or do, Mariah looked around for someone else who could make it better. But all the volunteer firemen were too busy, and none of Zeb's friends or neighbors seemed to be around. Even his dog seemed to have disappeared somewhere between town and here. She shook her head, feeling helpless. What did she know about comforting anyone?

Out of the corner of her eye, she glimpsed a flutter of white. Pivoting, she spotted a white-clad figure threading its way through the forest shadows. Mariah frowned. It almost looked like a young woman dressed in a long-sleeved white blouse and old-fashioned skirt. As Mariah stared harder, the young woman's edges seemed to waver and blur. Mariah blinked and rubbed her eyes. When she looked again, the figure had turned and was gazing straight back at her. Mariah's mouth dropped open. She recognized her. It was the girl she'd glimpsed in the mirror.

Mariah glanced over her shoulder to see if anyone else could see this apparition. But Zeb's back was facing her and no one else was paying her any attention. They were all focused on the fire. She slowly looked forward again, half expecting the girl in white to have vanished like she had back at the motel. But instead, the ghostly girl had drifted closer. She now stood at the edge of the woods, her lovely face wreathed in sorrow and desperation, as she lifted an imploring hand in Mariah's direction.

An answering ache rose up in Mariah's throat so strong it caught her by surprise. And she wanted to turn and run, not get involved, not feel this emotion she couldn't name. But something in the other girl's beseeching gaze held her fast. She didn't know what the girl wanted, but she knew she couldn't just walk away. Not in the face of such quiet pleading. She took a deliberate step toward the girl instead, closing the distance between them.

The young woman pointed to a gold locket around her neck and tried to speak. Her lips moved, but no sound came out.

Mariah shook her head. "I don't understand." She stepped even closer, moving from the sunlight and smoke surrounding Raven's Crossing into the shadows of the Hollows.

The young woman opened her locket. There were two photos inside. She pointed to the one on the left, a picture of a girl so similar in appearance they could be sisters. Once again she tried to speak. Her voice was silent, but her lips shaped two distinct words: Free her.

"Free her? Who?" Mariah asked.

The girl in white didn't answer. Instead, she lifted her hand and spread her fingers wide. Five. Her mouth moved again: Free them.

She tried to say something else, but she was starting to fade. The trees surrounding her seemed to press closer, their shadows enclosing her. And then, just like that, she was gone.

Mariah shivered. Her hands were ice-cold, her feet frozen in place. A ghost. She'd just had a conversation with a ghost. But one she did not understand. She stared hard into the Hollows, hoping to catch another glimpse of the apparition in white, but there was no sign of her. Only eerie silence and something else. Something unseen. Something frightening. Fear prickled across her skin.

Holding her breath, Mariah slowly backed away from the woods. She watched the spaces between the trees, afraid of what might leap out at her. When nothing moved, she turned and ran back into the sunshine. She had to tell Zeb what she had just seen. Maybe he would know what it meant.

But the fire chief reached him first. "It looks like the fire was contained to the one room," he said. "The rest of the house appears to be undamaged. If you'd like to go inside now..."

Zeb took off running before the man had finished. Not knowing what else to do, Mariah ran after him. She followed him inside, staying close on his heels as he crossed the formal front room and headed up the stairs. It wasn't until he reached the threshold of the tower room that his steps slowed. Mariah peered past his shoulder into the fairy tale room. Only now it looked like a scene from one of Grimm's horrific tales.

The walls were blackened, the windows broken; it stank of smoke and charred leather. Zeb shook his head, muttering something under his breath. The wet carpet squished under his feet as he crossed to the large desk in the center of the room. Mariah trailed after him, shocked by the destruction. It was as if a lightning storm had taken place in this room. There were dark marks on the floor and ceiling and torn bits of paper scattered across every surface.

Amid the ruins of the room, she spotted the corner of a sepia-toned photograph sticking out from under a burned book. She wanted to point it out to Zeb, but his attention was riveted on the desk. She stooped and picked it up instead. The photograph was covered in a fine coating of ash. She was starting to brush it away so she could see the face beneath when Zeb swore and kicked over a chair, startling her.

"This is a disaster!"

Mariah shoved the old-fashioned photograph into her pocket, out of sight.

"Do they know how it started?" she asked, turning to face him.

Zeb's face was grim as he shook his head. "They don't, but I have a pretty good idea."

With his finger, he drew a line through the thick ash and soot covering the desk. Then, eyes wide, he started frantically brushing away the rest of the burnt remnants until the top of the desk was clear. What he saw made him swear again.

"What is it?" Mariah asked.

"Looks like you're not the only one Kane is after," he said, moving aside so she could see the hate-filled words scorched into the wood.

VENGEANCE WILL BE MINE RAVEN.

Chapter Twelve

The Keeper

THE BOOKBAG ZEB HAD taken from the tower room at Raven's Crossing before the fire was tucked in the corner of his motel room. He pulled it out and spilled its contents on the table. The pile was pitifully small. If only he had taken more books with him. Better still, he should have started studying immediately following his dad's death. Regret swelled inside him as he ran his hand through his hair, overwhelmed by the immensity of the task he now faced. The loss of the library was too much to process.

"Can I get you a water or something?" Mariah asked.

Zeb jumped at the sound of her voice. He shook his head. The thought of drinking something right now made his stomach churn. He sat in a chair, picked up his father's Keeper journal, and thumbed through the pages. His eyes stung upon seeing the familiar handwriting, and Zeb inhaled slowly, fighting to get his emotions under control.

Mariah perched on the corner of his bed, and he could feel her eyes on him. He didn't want her there, and yet, he didn't want to be alone.

He ran his fingers over the pages of the book. His father made entries every year on the 11th of this month. Zeb paused to read.

Did the annual renewal of the wards today. All is well.

A chill raced through him. Annual renewal? He hadn't known about that, and he certainly hadn't done it. As much as he wanted to blame Mariah for her part in this, he was the Keeper. The Keeper who hadn't bothered to learn, who hadn't kept Grayhaven safe.

He slammed the journal down on the table, and a slim book slipped off the surface onto the floor. He didn't bother to pick it up.

"Can I do anything?" Mariah asked.

Zeb glared at her, his tone bitter. "Do you know how to set the wards?"

She shook her head.

"Well, that's what I need. You don't have to sit here and watch me. It's not helping."

"Fine. I'll leave." Mariah stooped to fix a shoelace and then hurried out the door before he could speak. It was probably for the best. He wasn't in the mood to deal with people right now.

Zeb paced the room. This mess was his fault, and he was the only one who could fix it. He sat back down and picked up the book of wards and spells. Notes were written in the margins. Some in his dad's handwriting, others in handwriting he didn't recognize. Keeper notes. He read through them, looking for anything that would tell him how to ward a grave. He found a drawing of a headstone and read the page carefully. Some Latin words, a candle. This seemed doable. He hoped that it would be this simple.

He grabbed a notebook from the desk drawer and scribbled the Latin words of the ritual on it. He'd get a candle from the stash in the motel office. Mariah had cracked Kane's headstone and Zeb guessed he would need to repair it. He hurried to the storage room where he kept tools and supplies. Rummaging on the back shelf, he found epoxy and stuffed it in a bag. He added a small container, a stir stick, a file, and duct tape. He slung the bag across his body and biked to Raven's Crossing.

As he approached the house, a hint of smoke lingered in the air. He didn't see anyone from the fire crew, only wet, trampled grass where they had stood, fighting the flames. Zeb hurried past the house. There would be plenty of time later for insurance adjusters and paperwork. Right now, he had to put Bartholomew Kane back where he belonged.

Zeb whistled hopefully, but Moose didn't appear. He passed the Raven headstones and paused. If only they were here to help. The true Keepers. A breeze licked his skin as he walked down the tree-lined path to the Hollows. "I am the Keeper. I can do this," he said softly. When he reached the iron gate, he squared his shoulders and entered the cemetery. Kane's headstone still stood eerily dark in the center of the cemetery. The crack Mariah made in the circle atop the stone was clearly visible in the afternoon light.

Entities pushed at the edge of his awareness. Restless. Testing the boundaries. Once Kane was back in place, Zeb knew he'd have to study his dad's journal and strengthen the wards for the whole cemetery before anything else broke free. He prayed everything would hold until then.

It didn't take long to mix the epoxy. Zeb daubed the mixture on the stone, filling the crack the best he could. He tried to force the ragged edges back together and then wrapped the headstone in duct tape to keep pressure on the crack while the epoxy set. It was a fast-setting mixture, but it would still take several hours to cure.

Zeb knelt before the headstone. He set a white candle at the base. The book indicated that if the ritual worked, the candle would light. "Here goes nothing," he said. He traced his fingers over the runes starting at the top and working his way down.

"Obfirmo. Restituo. Signo."

He sat back and waited. The candle remained unlit. He swore and tried again, speaking louder.

"Obfirmo. Restituo. Signo."

Close, restore, seal.

A tiny flame flickered at the tip of the candle wick. It wasn't very strong, but it was something. He hoped it was enough.

Before he could get to his feet, the duct tape began peeling away from the stone. The ripping sound of the tape being removed filled the air. He stared in horror as a barely visible hand unwound the tape. Zeb scrambled to his feet and glanced around for something, anything, he could use to stop what was happening. Seeing nothing, he swung at the ghostly hand, but his own hand passed right through it. He pressed the remaining tape to hold it in place but was knocked backward. The cold in the air took his breath away. He watched in complete helplessness as the last strip of tape came away from the stone and dropped harmlessly to the ground. The epoxy cracked, and as the gap in the headstone widened, the candle went out.

A twisted laugh came from the edge of the cemetery and the hair on his arms stood on end. Zeb grabbed the candle, stuffed everything in his bag, and stumbled out of the cemetery. He ran down the path toward the house. He'd failed. Maybe his dad was the last Keeper. It was tempting to hurry back to the motel, pack his things, and leave Grayhaven and the Hollows and all that resided there behind him.

He reached the family graves, shaky and out of breath. A voice broke the silence and Zeb froze. Was it Kane come back to torture him?

Moose appeared and lay down on his dad's grave, resting his head on his paws.

"Now you show up," Zeb said, his voice quavering. As a kid, he loved hearing stories about the arcane. But as an adult, he found those stories had lost their charm. What he was living was all too real. He stepped toward the big dog.

"Zeb, you have to finish this."

His Dad's voice. Clear and unmistakable. He spun around but couldn't see his father anywhere. Still, he could feel his presence, and it was the complete opposite of what he'd experienced in the cemetery. This presence was warm. Strong. Non-threatening. Zeb closed his eyes.

"I can't, Dad. I don't know what to do."

"You have what it takes, son."

"Dad?" His throat was tight. "Where are you?"

Only silence answered him. Moose came over and pushed his head under Zeb's hand, asking to be petted. Zeb scratched the dog's ear and blinked back tears.

He'd wanted to see his dad for so long, and now that it had happened, it had gone by so fast. Too fast. Zeb swallowed the lump in his throat.

His father knew what had happened in the Hollows, and yet Zeb didn't sense any blame or anger in the familiar voice. Zeb was the new Keeper, and his dad believed in him. Maybe it was time he started believing in himself.

Despite his inexperience, the ritual had almost worked. He had nearly pulled it off. There had to be a way to stop Kane, and he would be the one to find it.

CHAPTER THIRTEEN

HELLO, MERCY GRAY

MARIAH WOKE UP TO bright sunlight shining through the gap in the motel room curtains and grabbed her phone to check the time. Her stomach growled. Even if the second day of the Thimbleberry Festival had a pancake breakfast, she was pretty sure she'd missed it, and lunch as well. Too bad. That syrup was worth the wait in line. Mariah dressed quickly and texted the mechanic. He responded that he would meet her at the shop in an hour.

She fingered the worn leather of the slim book she'd taken from Zeb's room. She hadn't stolen it. Not really. It was more like borrowing. Last night, Zeb was visibly shaken by what happened, and she had to admit she felt a bit guilty for her part in it. Guilt was an unfamiliar emotion for her, and not one she enjoyed. She grabbed the book as she left her room. Maybe something in it would be of use.

The air was warm as Mariah walked toward town. She passed a park where mature trees shaded several picnic tables. It was quiet here. Mariah glanced at her phone. She still had a bit of time before the mechanic would be at the shop, so she sat at one of the tables and opened the book. The pages were discolored and filled with handwritten diary entries. She squinted at the smudgy ink.

15 December 1882

He asked again. I turned him down again. How many times must I reject him before he understands that I will never marry him? Emily says I must hold my ground and that eventually, he will stop asking. I hope she is right.

Intrigued, Mariah kept reading.

8 January 1883

Mr. Kane was here last night talking to Papa. I stayed out of sight in my room and read a book. Aurora and Mama were visiting Mrs. James, who has been under the weather. I think Aurora was hoping Thomas James was going to be home. Mr. Kane sounds angry with Papa. Something to do with the quarry. I'll feel better when he leaves. Or when Mama comes home. At least he hasn't asked for my hand again.

23 January 1883

Emily is dead. I was with her only two days ago, and now she is gone. No one can explain what happened. It is so unexpected. She was my friend, and I cannot believe I won't see her again.

26 January 1883

Yesterday was Emily's funeral. The doctor said her heart seemed paralyzed. It stopped, but Emily did not. Not for a time after. Her mother told me Emily's eyes were open and staring, and that she looked so frightened trying to breathe. It is horrifying, and everyone is praying that her illness is not some new plague in town.

We stopped by the Hansen home after the service. Mama brought stew and bread. So many people came to pay their respects. Even Bartholomew Kane. He gave me his handkerchief to dry my tears.

Mariah paused. Heart paralysis. She remembered seeing that in the town burial records. This book might not contain a spell to help Zeb, but it did talk about those mysterious deaths. Five, she recalled. All women.

14 February 1883

Jane was found dead. I heard a rumor at her funeral that she had a mark cut near her collarbone. Someone said Emily did, too. Is someone killing people in Grayhaven? Mama is hesitant to let me or Aurora go out. She did the shopping herself this week and wouldn't let us help. Aurora is not content to stay in and read, despite the winter cold. I know she is eager to see Thomas again.

26 February 1883

Everyone in Grayhaven is living under a cloud of fear. Three of my friends are dead. Murdered, according to the town gossip. Each lingering in a state of paralysis, each with a terrified look on their faces, each with a strange mark cut into their skin. It is the work of the devil, some say. Emily. Jane. Mary. All gone and buried now. Mama won't let me leave the house.

7 March 1883

Aurora and I have begun making up stories about people in town to pass the time. She has a keen sense of humor. She is good company, and not only my sister, but my best friend. I know she has sneaked out at least once to see Thomas. I made her promise not to do it again.

29 March 1883

A fourth death. Deborah. She was Aurora's age. I did not know her well.

11 April 1883

Aurora went out last night, and she has not returned home. I am sick with worry. Papa has gone in search of her. All I can do is wait. And pray.

13 April 1883

Aurora is...

dead.

The next few pages were blank. Mariah leafed through the book and stopped when she found a photograph tucked between the pages. It looked like a family photo. A couple and their teenaged children. The woman seated in front on the left side had a familiar face. A face she'd seen in the motel room mirror and at Raven's Crossing. She flipped the photo over. Ezekiel and Violet Gray, Mercy, Aurora, and John.

"Well hello, Mercy," she said, matching the name on the photo to the ghost she'd been seeing. In the photo, Aurora's eyes looked eager and alive. Mercy's were serene. When Mercy tried to communicate with her at the house, had she been talking about Aurora? Maybe Aurora was the girl in the locket. She pulled out the photograph that had survived the fire in the tower room. Wiping off the smoky sheen, she examined the faces. She didn't want to admit that ghosts were real, but she couldn't deny that she had seen Mercy. More than once.

This journal had been in Zeb's house, and she wondered what his connection was to the Gray family. If there wasn't a connection, how had he come into possession of this book? Mariah didn't think it was a coincidence that she'd been seeing the ghost, or that she'd found these photos. It had to have something to do with Bartholomew Kane. And now Mercy Gray was working hard to communicate with her.

Help them. Free them. Five.

Mariah shuddered as she flipped through the remaining pages of the diary. There were a few entries in different handwriting, as if the journal had been handed down in the family. She skimmed the pages. Nothing helpful, or of interest. But the last entry was different.

17 June 1923

Dearest John,

I cannot stay in Grayhaven any longer. You know I love you more than life itself, but I feel in my soul that whatever came and took our sweet Sarah will come for Rachel, too. This town...your family...it feels like a curse. I cannot bear to lose Rachel. I have to keep her safe. I'm sorry to leave you this way, but you know it is for the best. Please come as soon as you can. I'll light a candle for you every night until you join us.

All my love,

Matilda

Mercy had a brother named John, according to the family photo. This entry must be about him. John and Matilda Gray. She remembered seeing their names at the Grayhaven cemetery. They were listed on the headstone for their infant daughter, Sarah. Tragedy certainly followed this family.

As Mariah tucked the photos into the diary, something tugged at the edge of her thoughts. The tree drawing from Fleur. What if it were a family tree? And the M. Could it have stood for Mercy? Or Matilda? The drawing was packed in her bags on the motorcycle. She'd look at it after she picked up her bike.

She tucked the diary inside her jacket and headed for Main Street and the center of town. As she passed the library, she noticed that the flowers were brown. Dead. She continued toward the plaza. People milled about, shopping at the vendor booths. A singer performed on the stage. Aside from the downed statue, little damage remained from the morning windstorm. The plants, however, told a different story. The windstorm had turned the lawn yellow and all the flowers brown.

She continued walking toward the auto shop, where all the plants were healthy and colorful. It was as if a boundary radiated out from the center of town and stopped here. Mariah still didn't want to think about Kane as the cause of all of this, nor did she like to think about the ghost she'd been seeing. But something was definitely wrong in Grayhaven.

Her bike was sitting out in front of the shop. The mechanic came out with her keys. "I couldn't find anything wrong with it," he said. "Runs like a dream."

Mariah bit her lip in frustration. She ran her hand over the bike and noticed a symbol carved in the pristine paint. "Did you do this? It wasn't there before."

The man bent over and rubbed at the spot with his cloth. The rune, or whatever it was, disappeared.

He shrugged. "It looks fine now."

But as Mariah watched, the rune returned. Was this why she couldn't leave town? She rubbed at it with her hand, and once more, it disappeared. It wasn't scratched into the paint. She took her keys and hopped on the bike, grateful to hear the engine rumble to life.

"You dropped this." The mechanic held out a photograph.

Mercy and Aurora. She was certain she'd secured that photo in the diary and couldn't imagine how it ended up here on the ground. Unless.... That Mercy Gray was one persistent ghost.

Mariah thanked the man and put on her helmet. She eased her bike out onto the road. She'd find Zeb and tell him that she was seeing a ghost. One with an agenda in mind.

CHAPTER FOURTEEN

THE PLOT THICKENS

GOOD EATS WAS SLAMMED. Zeb couldn't remember the last time so many people had come into the diner. Guess that's what came of having half the power out in Grayhaven. And as good as Carlos was at manning the grill, not even he could handle this many customers by himself. Which was why Zeb was refilling water glasses, delivering plates of food, busing tables, and taking orders instead of researching another way to contain Bartholomew Kane before he wreaked even more havoc in Grayhaven. But after struggling to decipher the first Keeper's handwritten journal for over two hours earlier that afternoon, he needed a break; he'd go back to it when the dinner rush was done. Maybe Moose would show up by then, too. The hound always seemed to make himself scarce when there were too many people around.

"Two double bacon cheeseburgers and a large order of chili fries," he called to Carlos. The stocky dark-haired man cheerfully lifted his hand in acknowledgement. *And a heart attack waiting to happen,* Zeb thought to himself as he started clearing the counter. Not that he didn't love a good bacon cheeseburger himself. Bacon made everything better.

He felt the warm press of a woman's body behind him and tensed. Then he heard Mariah's breathless voice in his ear. "I have to show you something."

Flushing, he turned around. Her beautiful amber eyes were shining in a way that made his breath catch. She held up a slim leatherbound book that looked vaguely familiar. "I was reading in this book and I figured out who she is."

"She who?" he frowned. What was she talking about?

Mariah leaned closer and Zeb felt his pulse speed up. "The ghost I've been seeing."

His brain stuttered to a stop. "Ghost? What ghost?"

"At your house..."

Dishes clanked on the counter behind them. "Plates up!" Carlos called out.

Mariah jumped and Zeb bit back a curse. "I'll be right back," he told her.

He delivered the plates of burgers and chili fries to the two guys sitting in the front booth, refilled their drinks, and slapped down their checks. He gave the rest of the diner a quick scan to make sure no one else needed anything. Then he hurried back to the counter where Mariah was waiting.

"Let's go over there," he said, pointing at a booth in the corner that had just been vacated. "Hey Carlos, I'm taking five."

Carlos looked over, eyed Mariah for a second, then grinned and gave Zeb a knowing wink. "Take ten. Or twenty. I got you covered."

Zeb studiously avoided looking at Mariah as he led the way to the empty table. Sitting down across from her, he tried to laugh it off. "Sorry 'bout that."

Mariah glanced around the crowded diner and frowned. "Why are there so many people here tonight?"

Zeb grimaced. "The power's out all over Grayhaven. We're one of the only places still open."

"That sucks." Then, as if realizing how her words sounded, she clapped a hand over her mouth. "I mean it sucks about the power being out," she stammered. "Not about your diner ...."

Zeb's mouth quirked. "I knew what you meant." Her cheeks pinkened as her eyes met his then quickly shifted away. Before it could get even more awkward, Zeb said, "So you were saying something about seeing a ghost?"

"I've seen her twice now. Once at the motel, and once out at your house." And she told him all about it, from what the ghost looked like to what she had tried to communicate. Mariah plunked the book she'd been holding onto the table and all at once Zeb recognized it. It was one of the books he'd retrieved from his dad's study before the fire.

"Where did you get that?"

"From you," Mariah said.

"You stole one of my books?"

"Borrowed," Mariah corrected, her thumb worrying at the lotus tattoo on her wrist. "I wanted to see if there was any useful information in it." She flipped it open and showed him the diary entries. "Mercy Gray wrote these. She knew Bartholomew Kane," she said. Then she pulled out two photographs. She pointed to the first one. "This is Mercy. She's the ghost I've been seeing. And this is her sister, Aurora."

"Aurora Gray?" The name clicked in Zeb's brain. He'd read Aurora's name in the first Keeper's journal. "She was Kane's last victim."

Mariah's eyes widened. "Bartholomew Kane killed Mercy's sister? But I thought he was in love with Mercy."

Zeb fingered the faded photograph of the two sisters. "Her father was sure he did it. And Aurora wasn't Kane's only victim. Kane killed five girls in all. They all had the same mark cut into their skin. Like some kind of ritual killing." He put the photo down and leaned back in the booth, feeling a sudden wave of sadness and regret that the Gray sisters' youthful beauty and innocence had been cut short by such evil. "The journal I read said that Ezekial

Gray and the other girls' fathers hunted Kane down and put an end to the killings."

"Shot until dead," Mariah murmured.

Zeb nodded. "They and Mathias Raven, my 4th great grandfather who became the first Keeper, buried Kane in that cemetery in the Hollows and set wards to bind his soul to keep him there forever."

Mariah shifted uneasily in her seat and Zeb clamped his mouth shut, not wanting to remind her again of what she'd done. But his silence must have come across as an accusation because she refused to look at him. Which made him feel bad. Because he wasn't mad at her anymore. He just didn't know what to say to make her feel better. And he sure as hell didn't know what to do about Kane or the ghost Mariah was seeing. But maybe he and Mariah could figure it out together. He leaned forward across the booth.

"Mariah, look, I'm sorry for yelling at you before. I know you didn't know what would happen."

"Zeb! I've been looking for you." The lilting interruption was accompanied by a cloud of floral scent. Zeb fought off a sneeze as he turned to greet Fleur. She gave him and Mariah a bright red-lipped smile. "It's so nice to see the two of you together," she said. She dug into her butterfly tote bag and pulled out a piece of paper. Smoothing the creased corners, she placed a sketch of an ornate dagger in front of Zeb. "This is for you," she said. Then she swiveled the sketch so it faced Mariah, and her smile faded away.

"It's for you, too, dear. But be careful with it, it cuts both ways." The silver rings on her fingers glinted as she placed her hand on Zeb's forearm and gave him an encouraging squeeze before leaving them with the sketch.

"I hate when she does that," Mariah said with a little shiver. "Someone needs to put a bell on her or something so you have some kind of warning before she hands you your doom."

Zeb chuckled. "Fleur takes her gift seriously."

"It's creepy," Mariah insisted. "I mean look at this," she said, shoving Fleur's sketch of the knife across the table at Zeb. "What is this? And why is she giving it to you?"

"To both of us," he reminded her. He studied the line-drawing of the strangely decorated dagger with a frown. "I think it's an athame."

"An atha-what?"

"It's a special kind of dagger used in spellcasting and other rituals."

"Like ritual killings?" Mariah asked.

Troubled, Zeb touched the silver amulet at his throat. It pulsed with cold fire, shocking his fingertips. He gazed down at Fleur's drawing, wishing he knew what it meant. Or what to do about it.

"You two kids got room for one more?" Jerry asked, shuffling up to their table. "Business sure is booming tonight."

"The power out at your place, too?" Zeb asked, standing to make room for him.

The old man shook his head. "Naw. I just didn't want to miss out on all the excitement."

Mariah snorted.

"Have a seat, Jerry. I'll go grab you a cup of coffee," Zeb said. He reached for the sketch as the old man slid into the booth, but Jerry grabbed it first.

"Is this that knife they found under old Ezekial Gray?" he asked.

Zeb frowned, trading glances with Mariah. "What knife?"

Jerry pulled the town's daily news sheet from his back pocket and unrolled it. He pointed to the top article. "It's right here," he said. "There was a hollowed-out spot beneath the statue and when it toppled over this morning, they found a knife hidden inside."

Zeb felt a frisson of excitement shoot through his body. This is what Fleur's sketch was trying to tell them; they needed this athame. He looked over at Mariah and saw the same realization in her eyes. She slipped out of the booth and gripped his arm. He nodded.

"What did they do with the knife?" he asked.

Jerry squinted at them. "The mayor said she was going to lock it up at the museum until they could figure out where it came from. Why?"

"No reason," Zeb said. "You want a sandwich or anything with your coffee?"

"Just my usual," Jerry said.

"One BLTC coming up," Zeb said. Taking Mariah by the arm, he steered her away from the table. "We need that knife," he murmured."

"You think it belonged to Kane?"

He closed his fist around his silver amulet, which still burned with an unnatural cold, and nodded. "Know anyone who can pick a lock?"

Mariah grinned in reply.

Chapter Fifteen

A Little B & E

Zeb stifled a big yawn. It had been a long day, and it wasn't over yet. He and Mariah had decided to wait until close to midnight before heading to the museum to make sure no one would be around to spot them breaking in. Not that they were planning on breaking anything. They just needed that knife.

"The coast looks clear," Mariah whispered.

Zeb looked up and down Spring Lane. No cars coming and no one in sight. They'd heard music coming from the town square earlier, but it was quiet now. And though there were lights on in a few houses around town, most of the houses in this neighborhood were still dark. Which was good for them.

He nodded. "Let's go."

The Historical Museum of Grayhaven was housed in a small white house with a stone porch and a faded sign hanging above the front door. As they crossed the front lawn, a dark shape rose out of the shadows to meet them. Mariah let out a surprised cry, but Zeb stepped forward with a grin.

"Hey, Moose! Where have you been?"

The hound greeted him with a happy wag of his tail.

Mariah approached the dog warily. "How'd he know where we'd be?"

"Moose always knows," he said, scratching behind the dog's ears. Moose woofed in agreement.

"So, he's some kind of psychic dog?" Mariah asked.

Zeb shrugged. "It's hard to explain. He's .... Moose."

Mariah shook her head, circled around the two of them, and climbed the three broad steps leading up to the museum's front door. "Zeb?" she asked.

"I'm coming," he said.

He gave Moose's head one last pat and jogged after her. The hound sat down on the edge of the lawn, content to keep watch from outside. Joining Mariah on the front porch, Zeb tried the door's brass handle. It was locked. He looked over at Mariah.

"How do we do this?"

With a mischievous grin, Mariah held up a set of lock picks. "Watch and learn," she said. She bent over the lock and got to work. In less than a minute she had the door open. "After you."

"That's amazing," Zeb said. "Where'd you learn to do that?"

Her smile seemed to dim as she turned away, tucking her lock picks back into her jacket pocket. "Just something I picked up in my wild misspent youth."

"Lucky for us," he said.

There was a story there, Zeb could tell. But even though he'd only known Mariah for a few days, he'd already learned that she guarded her past like iron and salt guarded against ghosts. She was prickly and tough and disarmingly beautiful. Especially when she let her guard down and smiled. And he was beyond glad she was in this thing with him. Clicking on his flashlight, he led the way into the museum.

The front room was strewn with shadows and the wooden floors creaked under their feet. Moonlight fell on the donation box near the stone fireplace. Zeb shone his flashlight around the room as Mariah closed the door behind them. There was an original map of Grayhaven hanging over the fireplace and a display case of tools from the old stone quarry off to the left. But no athame.

"Hey, look at this," Mariah said. She'd crossed to the display case on the opposite wall and was using the light of her phone to study the contents inside. She pointed to an old cookbook. "Here's the original recipe for thimbleberry syrup."

"Any silver daggers?"

"Just some hand-carved buttons and a set of ladles."

Zeb flicked his flashlight over the display case with a frown, then surveyed the rest of the room. Where would they have put the athame? He pointed to the back of the museum. "Why don't you go check the displays in there while I go check out the office?"

"Sure thing," Mariah said, looking a little too comfortable in her role of thief. Zeb kept feeling a guilty need to glance over his shoulder to make sure no one was about to catch them in the act.

"Yell if you find anything," he said. And they split up.

Mariah disappeared into the next room and Zeb skirted the round table loaded with books and postcards for sale and headed toward the back of the museum. The office door was closed but not locked. He let himself in, letting the light of his flashlight play around the room. There were two file cabinets by the door, a couple of chairs, a rolltop desk against one wall, and a corner computer desk and copy machine against the other.

"If I were an athame, where would I be?" he asked.

He started with the file cabinets, but the drawers were crammed with files and papers; he found two old phones in the bottom drawer, but no knife. Next, he crossed to the desk. He checked the center and side drawers first with no luck, then rolled back the slatted top. And there it was, lying in the exact center of the flat writing surface, wrapped up in an off-white linen napkin.

Heart beating fast, Zeb set his flashlight down and carefully unwrapped the knife. It was about twelve inches long and heavy, with a hand-carved ebony handle and a double-edged silver blade that shimmered even in the faint light. Inset near the top of the handle was a deep red carnelian crystal. Some kind of inscription was etched down the center of the blade. It was a lethal weapon, but there was a dark beauty to it, too. Still, Zeb hesitated to touch it with his bare hands. Kane had used this blade to kill five young women. And that kind of evil left an imprint.

Rewrapping the athame in the linen square, Zeb went to find Mariah. He spotted her slender form in the middle of the darkened museum near a mannequin dressed in a long silk ballgown from another era. She was bent over a glass case and it almost looked like she had opened it. Or was that just a trick of the moonlight and shadows? She straightened when she saw him coming.

"What were you doing?" he asked, glancing at the case. It held a pair of white gloves and a lacy fan and nothing else.

Mariah shoved her hands in her pockets. "Just checking out this case." She nodded at the bundle in his hands. "Is that it?"

"There's something written on the blade," Zeb said. And he unrolled the cloth to show her. She held up her lit phone to get a better look.

"What does it say?"

Zeb leaned closer. The blade seemed to absorb the phone's light, making the dark inscription even harder to read. He tilted the blade to try and see the words from another angle, and suddenly the words etched in the silver athame were all too clear.

"Whoso spilleth blood with this blade claimeth the souls of the dead."

"Claimeth their souls?" Mariah asked, her amber eyes wide. "Does that mean Kane didn't just kill those girls?"

"He took their souls," Zeb said. The thought filled him with horror. Kane was more than a murderer; he was a stealer of souls. But why? Was it because he gained some kind of supernatural power from them? And what was his end game? Zeb shuddered, feeling sick to his stomach. Kane was truly evil. And those poor girls! Had they really been trapped with that evil for all of these years?

Mariah looked as horror-stricken as he felt. She grabbed his arm so tight it hurt. "That's what Mercy meant when she told me to free them. We have to help them, Zeb. We have to free their souls!"

Chapter Sixteen

Spirit Traps and Amulets

When Mariah entered the Good Eats Diner, she spotted Zeb seated at a nearby table and headed toward him.

"We need a ghost trap," he said before she was even seated.

"Good morning to you, too. What's a ghost trap?" she yawned. All the adrenaline released last night left her feeling tired today.

"A ghost trap is exactly what it sounds like. We need to summon Kane and free the souls of those women. If we trap him, we can put him back in the cemetery. That's how we fix this."

Despite the dark circles under his mismatched eyes, Zeb was different this morning. He exuded a confidence she hadn't seen in him before, and the energy around him was contagious. She felt her layers of fatigue melt away as he talked.

"Someone's been doing some research," she said. "Did you sleep at all?"

"Not much."

Moose padded over and sat by Zeb, gazing up at him with a hopeful expression. When Zeb ignored him, Moose nudged Mariah on the leg and whined.

"Sorry, pal. I don't have any food," she said. The dog moved away, snuffling around the floor and searching under the tables.

"And you know how to summon Kane and make a ghost trap?" she asked.

"I think so. And I have most of what I need right here. I just need to figure out the right location, and we'll be set."

Moose returned, an empty food bowl in his mouth. He dropped the bowl on the floor near Zeb where it wobbled before settling with one last thud. Zeb stood up so fast he jostled the table. "Sorry, Moose!" He grabbed the bowl and headed for the kitchen.

"Well, that got his attention," Mariah said. Moose laid his head on her leg and half-closed his eyes while she stroked his silky ears. She didn't know what had changed, exactly, between her and the rangy hound, but she had to admit they were warming up to each other.

Zeb returned with a heaping bowl of food. He'd barely set it on the floor before Moose began gulping down the contents. "Yesterday was so crazy, I missed his dinner."

Moose raised his head ran his tongue over his jowls before returning his attention to the bowl.

"I think you're forgiven," Mariah said. Moose finished eating, and she had to admit she was jealous of the dog's full stomach.

"Coffee?" Zeb asked. "I made a fresh pot."

She shook her head. "I could eat something, though."

"Carlos is coming in a bit late after the dinner rush last night. I'll grab us something." He rose and went to the kitchen, and she had to admit his jeans fit him rather well.

Zeb returned with pastries and juice. "Care to walk into town? I can't borrow Carlos's truck since he's not here."

She shook her head as she picked up a muffin. "My motorcycle works great as long as we stay in Grayhaven. We can ride double." She wasn't about to walk when she could ride.

A rosy tint colored Zeb's cheeks, and Mariah found it oddly endearing. Grayhaven might not be Hallmark material, but Zeb definitely had his own small-town charm. She had to admit he was growing on her.

They finished eating and Zeb followed her outside. The sky was filled with low-hanging gray clouds, and she smelled a hint of rain in the air. Zeb stood near the bike, and she sensed his hesitation. "Here, you take the helmet. Where are we heading?"

"Stone Quarry Jewelry. It's not far from the library," he said. "They'll be open in a few minutes."

She swung her leg over the bike as he fumbled with the helmet.

"It's not a big seat," she said. "You'll have to sit close so you don't fall off the backside. And you'd better hold on to my waist."

He got on behind her and placed his hands gingerly on her waist. Heat from his touch warmed her skin through the thin layer of her t-shirt. First Moose cozied up to her, and now this. Mariah turned the ignition, but even the familiar grumble of the engine coming to life couldn't distract her from the unexpected comfort of having Zeb in close proximity. Perhaps she'd been riding solo for too long.

When they arrived at the shop, Mariah followed Zeb. The bell over the door jangled as they entered.

"Be right with you," the man behind the counter said.

Mariah glanced at a rack of postcards near the doorway. Two or three were in full color, shots of what she guessed must be the quarry, and of Main Street. The other postcards were of old buildings, all printed in sepia tone. She joined Zeb at the counter as he pulled at a chain around his neck. He showed the man the amulet.

"I need one of these," he said.

The man frowned. "I'm sorry, Zeb. I sold out at the Thimbleberry Festival. Do you want me to call you when I have more?"

Zeb fingered the amulet. "No chance of a rush job? Or that you have a stray in the back?"

"Let me look. Hold tight."

Mariah pointed to the amulet. "Yours not working?"

Zeb tucked it back beneath his shirt. "Mine works fine, but I figure you could use one with Kane on the loose. It's an old design that Keepers have been using for years for added protection. This one was my dad's. He was the Keeper before me."

Mariah wasn't used to having someone concerned about her welfare. Not knowing how to respond, she focused on the rest of what Zeb had said. He was a Keeper? She pictured the graves behind Raven's Crossing. All men. All Ravens. If Zeb was the latest in a long line of Keepers, it explained why he felt responsible to protect everyone from Bartholomew Kane.

The man returned and shook his head. "Sorry, I didn't find one."

Zeb thanked him and they turned to leave. As Mariah approached the door, postcards began flying off the rack. She stumbled backward and Zeb caught her, his arm around her waist, steadying her. Her heart thudded against her ribs, and she shivered. Was it Kane again?

The cards swirled in the air for a moment and then dropped, face up, onto the floor. Mariah slipped out of Zeb's grasp and bent to pick up a card. The images were all the same—a sepia-toned photograph of an old Victorian house. She stood up and saw a figure near the rack.

Mercy Gray.

The woman gestured at the card and put her hand to her chest. *Grave*, she mouthed.

"Grave?" Mariah asked, her voice barely above a whisper. "Yours?"

Mercy nodded as she faded from the room.

"Was that Mercy?" Zeb asked.

"You saw her?"

"Yes. You look like her. The eyes...and the mouth."

Mariah ignored him. She did *not* look like a ghost. She flipped over the postcard and read the back. "Home of Ezekiel Gray. Do you know this place?"

"Everyone in Grayhaven does," Zeb said. "Why?"

"I think Mercy wants us to go to her grave."

Zeb picked up the postcards, stacked them neatly, and returned them to the rack. "Makes sense. Kane was in love with Mercy. She's telling us where to set the trap."

Once back at the motel office, Zeb handed her a canvas bag. "Here, hold this."

Opening a cupboard, he pulled out a glass jar with a lid, a round mirror, a black candle, salt, and rue. Zeb wrapped the mirror and glass jar in small towels and placed everything in the bag. He opened the Keeper's manual that rested on the counter and ran his finger down the page, his mouth moving as he read the words. He frowned and read the page again. Slamming the book closed in frustration, he let out a groan.

"What is it?" Mariah asked.

"We need a personal item tied to the site where we're setting the trap."

"Something connected to Mercy?"

Zeb ran a hand through his hair, standing part of it up on end. "Yes, I think that would work. But she's been dead a hundred years. Where are we going to find something?"

Mariah reached into her pocket and pulled out a locket on a chain. "Try this."

Zeb took the locket from her and opened it. She saw recognition flash across his face as he saw two photos inside. One of Mercy Gray and one of her sister, Aurora.

"How did you get this?"

"I found it last night" she began.

He raised a hand and stopped her. "You took this from the museum? You have to quit doing that!" he said. But he grinned. "I'm glad you have it. This is perfect to summon him. It'll work best if we set the trap during a between-time, like twilight. Not day anymore, but not quite night."

She took the necklace back from him. "I'll bring the locket, you bring the athame, and we'll have a little date with Mr. Kane," Mariah said. A chill ran through her, and she wondered if the ghost were near. If he could hear them planning. Her stomach fluttered in anticipation. This would be her biggest job yet.

CHAPTER SEVENTEEN

THE SUMMONING

THUNDER RUMBLED AS ZEB walked past Ezekiel Gray's house, leading Mariah toward the private cemetery. The Victorian house was eerily quiet now that it was closed for the evening. Zeb remembered touring it once in elementary school, but he hadn't been inside since.

A droplet of rain splashed on his cheek, and he brushed it away. That was the last thing he needed, rain while he tried to summon a ghost. He glanced up at the heavy, menacing clouds, and willed them to hold off on releasing their load.

"Do you suppose rain goes right through ghosts?" Mariah asked, her voice breaking the tension building inside him.

"Hadn't thought about it," he said, grateful for her presence. He'd never tried to do anything like this before, and he didn't relish facing Kane alone.

They reached the white picket fence that formed a rectangle at the edge of the property. Most of the Gray family were buried elsewhere, but two graves lay within the enclosure. He paused and heard Mariah's sharp intake of breath as she stopped beside him.

"Mercy and Aurora," she said softly. "It makes it all real, seeing this."

"Do you see Mercy anywhere?" he asked.

She glanced around. "No."

A flash of lightning made them both jump and Zeb counted silently as he waited for the thunder. The low grumble rolled toward him from a distance. "Let's do this," he said, and opened the gate.

He took a can of orange spray paint from the bag and hesitated.

"What are you waiting for?" Mariah asked.

"It feels wrong to desecrate their graves."

"Want me to do it?" She reached for the can. "Or is it something only a Keeper can do?"

He thrust the paper with the design he'd copied painstakingly from a Keeper journal at her. "I think it'll work if you do it."

She took the page and studied it, shaking the can. She walked to the foot of the graves and stood on a patch of ground between them. Popping off the lid, she sprayed an orange circle about three feet in diameter. Her brow furrowed as she made a smaller circle inside the first and connected the two with lines radiating outward like spokes on a wheel. It was delicate work to spray the rune in the inner circle, and to make the correct symbols in each section around it.

"Picking locks and spray painting—what other hidden talents do you have?" Zeb asked.

Mariah raised an eyebrow. "Stick around and you might find out," she said.

Was she flirting with him? He wouldn't mind if she was. He also wouldn't mind if she decided to stay in Grayhaven for a bit after all of this was over.

"I just might do that," Zeb said.

Mariah capped the spray can and handed it back to him. Was it his imagination, or had her hand lingered when it touched his?

He arranged the things they needed near the edge of the circle: the jar, the black candle, and the mirror. He held out the jar lid where Mariah could see it and showed her the rune on the bottom.

"That should hold him once we get him in the jar," Zeb said. He placed the lid on the ground. "Do you have the locket?"

Mariah took it out of her pocket and handed it to him. Zeb opened the locket and placed the pendant and chain on the symbol in the center of the circle. Mercy and Aurora stared up at him from the open locket. Out of the corner of his eye, he saw Mariah flinch as a raindrop landed on Mercy's face. He needed to hurry before the rain grew worse.

Zeb stood at the foot of Mercy's grave at the edge of the spray-painted circle. "You stand by Aurora's grave," he said.

Mariah took her place. A gust of wind whipped the blue strands of her hair into her face. She tucked the strands behind her ear. Zeb lifted the amulet from beneath his shirt, letting it rest against his chest. He reached for Mariah's hand and clasped it firmly in his own. Her hand was warm, and the contact was soothing.

"Whatever happens, don't let go," he said.

"I won't."

Something shimmered on the opposite side of the circle, near the head of the graves. A woman took form, wearing a high-necked white blouse and a long skirt. He recognized her from the locket photo and from the shop. Mercy Gray. Her face was filled with hope, and he found it reassuring that she was there, willing them to succeed. Mercy raised a hand and gestured at him, as if she were impatient for him to begin. Zeb lifted his face to the clouds, ignoring the raindrops splashing on his skin as he shouted into the storm.

"Within this circle be contained, I summon thee, Bartholomew Kane!"

Thunder crashed and Zeb gripped Mariah's hand as rain poured from the sky. Blinding light filled the air, and the hairs on his arms stood up. He could smell burning, like melted electrical wire.

And then, Kane was there, larger than life. Zeb sensed, rather than saw him. A presence that filled the circle and commanded attention. The ghost grew more distinct, his form tall and threatening. Evil emanated from the circle, and Zeb felt Mariah's grip loosen. He held onto her, not letting her slip away. Zeb edged away from the circle, creating a little more space between him and Kane. Mariah copied his movement and, to his relief, held his hand firmly once again

"Now what?" Mariah called out over the thunder. Rain showered down, soaking them.

"We free the women," Zeb said. He pulled the athame from his belt and raised it toward the menacing figure. The blade felt wrong in his hand, dark and yearning, as if it wanted to be reunited with Kane. Zeb tightened his grip.

"With this blade he claimed your souls, and with this blade I set you free."

Zeb's hand trembled as he held the knife, but he knew what he had to do. Raising the athame, he slashed at the dark shape of Bartholomew Kane. A roar filled the air, driving him backward even as the knife pulled toward the spirit. He held onto both the athame and Mariah as a small light shivered away from Kane and hovered beyond the summoning circle that contained him.

Zeb repeated the statement and drove the athame again and again. Two more lights left the circle, and Kane's presence became narrower, shrunken. Kane grimaced; his mouth twisted in his gaunt face. The ghost was losing power with each soul he freed. The athame felt more comfortable in his hand as if the heavy darkness that infused it was also dissipating.

Kane reached for him. As the ghostly hand clawed at his wrist, cold shot up his arm, through his shoulder, toward his heart. Fear filled him. *I can't do this. He'll take me. He's too powerful.* Every instinct inside him screamed for him to run, but he couldn't move. Couldn't speak. Energy drained from him, and his legs shook. Was this how those girls felt when Kane took their souls?

"Zeb?" Mariah squeezed his hand. Her voice shook him out of his paralysis. His amulet glowed as a line of light ran from it down his arm to the blade. He drew strength from the light and straightened, standing tall in the rain. He was the Keeper, and he would not back down now.

Zeb swung at the ghost with a stabbing motion, but he was not quick enough. Kane dodged easily, moving in the confines of the circle. Zeb shifted, studying the ghost.

"How many?" Zeb shouted. He had lost track.

"Three," she said.

Kane swung his gaze toward Mariah and Zeb took advantage, plunging the knife at the ghost. He caught Kane on the arm, and the ghost howled in fury as another light broke free and slipped outside the circle.

"That's four! You're almost done," Mariah said.

Kane glared at him with sunken eyes, focused on Zeb's every move. The ghost of Mercy Gray paced between the graves, beyond the circle, beyond the reach of Kane. Her nervous energy urged him on. One more soul to free. The one Mercy cared about the most. Aurora was the last girl taken, and now, she would be the last to be freed. He was determined to finish the task.

Zeb focused on the amulet resting against his shirt. It glowed brighter, and he drew every ounce of strength he could from it. He raised the knife one more time, and feinted left. When Kane dodged, Zeb plunged the knife to the right, catching the ghost on the arm.

"With this blade that claimed you, I free you, Aurora Gray!"

A loud clap of thunder sounded, and Kane's anger reverberated through Zeb's chest like a deep, thrumming bass note as the last soul broke free. Five lights flew from the circle toward Mercy, and she stepped between them and Kane. Zeb saw her standing tall and unflinching in the face of Kane's wrath. She had a little smile on her face as she looked beyond Kane to Zeb.

Four women clustered behind her, but the fifth, Aurora, took shape next to her. Mercy flung her arms around her sister and held her tight. Warmth filled him. Gratitude from Mercy, Aurora, and the others. For the first time, he had a taste of both the sacrifice and the reward, and he understood what it meant to be a Keeper.

The rain was letting up, and light from the rising moon peeked out beneath the clouds in the evening sky. Four of the ghosts faded away, and only the Gray sisters remained. Mercy raised her hand to her heart in a gesture of gratitude.

"You did it," Mariah said.

Kane howled and lunged at her, and Zeb raised the athame. Kane retreated to the center of the circle.

The job was not yet finished. The girls were free, but the summoning circle would not hold Kane forever, and while the ghost no longer looked threatening, now a shadow of his former self, Zeb knew that looks could be deceiving. He needed to get Kane in the ghost trap and back to the Hollows.

"We're not done yet. Get the jar," he said, releasing Mariah's hand. He kept the athame pointed at the ghost. It was no longer Kane's weapon.

Kane lunged again and Zeb felt his presence pushing at the barrier created by the circle. The boundary line began to give way.

"Light the candle!" Zeb shouted. "Light it now!"

Chapter Eighteen

Ghost Trapping

For a moment Mariah couldn't tear her gaze away from Mercy and her sister. Though faint and fading fast, she could still see the ethereal halo of light encircling them. It stood in stark contrast to the darkness of Kane's own spirit, shrunken but not gone. Zeb was standing between her and Kane, keeping the ghost's malevolent energy at bay with the athame. The jar, mirror and black candle for the spirit trap lay at his feet.

A small dust devil spun to life within the summoning circle, powered by Kane's rage, pelting her and Zeb with small rocks and twigs. Shielding her face, Mariah knelt. She made sure the black candle was centered on the mirror in the bottom of the jar, careful not to smudge Kane's initials or the special rune Zeb had so painstakingly drawn on the glass and reached for the matches. But the rain had started up again and the first match she lit quickly fizzled out. She grabbed another. Striking it, she cupped her left hand around the flickering flame, but before she could light the candle, the match once again went out. Another crack of thunder made her duck. When she looked up, Kane was staring right at her. She trembled beneath the weight of his sinister glare.

"Hurry up, Mariah," Zeb called. "I don't know how long the circle will hold."

"I can't get the candle lit!" she cried, unable to hide the growing panic in her voice.

Zeb slashed at Kane with the knife, forcing the ghost to shrink back. Then he dropped down beside her. Unzipping his sweatshirt, he held it over her to shelter her from the spatter of raindrops. Mariah heard Kane's growl of rage as she struck a third match. It lit! With shaking hands, she reached inside the jar and held it to the black candle. When the wick flamed up hot and bright she almost cried.

"Here, hold this," Zeb said, handing her the athame. He picked up the jar and its lid and turned to face Bartholomew Kane.

Mariah stood next to him. The seething oily smoke of Kane's soul solidified in the center of the summoning circle, giving him shape once more. Kane's fearsome visage focused again on Mariah. His dead black gaze bored into her soul.

"You bitch! You're just like her." His voice was like barbwire. "Gray blood runs true even in you."

Fear like she'd never known before coursed through her body. She almost dropped the knife. Zeb swung the ghost trap between her and Kane. The glow of the candle's flame drew Kane's gaze.

"Quick, Mariah," Zeb said. "Break the circle."

She scraped at the orange circle spraypainted on the ground with the point of the athame until there was a distinct gap in it. Kane raked the air above her head; his misshapen fingernails looked like twisted black claws. It would only take one swipe to draw blood. Mariah flinched as he reached across the summoning circle for her. But the pull of the ghost trap was too strong. The glint of mirror and flame drew him in, and the seething blackness of his soul poured into the jar. He howled with rage as Zeb clapped the lid inscribed with runes on tight, trapping the ghost inside. For a moment, neither of them moved. Then Zeb turned to Mariah with an expression of disbelief on his face.

"We did it," he exclaimed. "We trapped Bartholomew Kane!"

Mariah couldn't help herself, she threw her arms around Zeb's neck in an exuberant hug. The rain on his skin was cool against her face. She couldn't believe they'd fought a ghost and won. She felt the press of the jar in Zeb's arms against her stomach. The glass was hot. It rocked violently against her midriff, and she let go of Zeb and quickly took a step backwards.

"Is that Kane?"

Zeb held the jar more securely against his chest. "He's trying to get out."

"Can he do that?" Mariah asked, trying not to sound as frightened as she suddenly felt.

"I don't know. I've never trapped a ghost before."

"But the jar will hold, right?"

Zeb threw her a crooked grin. "It should. At least until we get it back to the cemetery in the Hollows."

Mariah eyed the jar warily. The candle inside had gone out, smothered by Kane's dark soul. Overhead, the storm clouds shifted and for a moment the patter of rain on her head stopped. She nodded. "Let's get this done."

Scooping up both the athame and Mercy's locket from the ground, she headed for the front drive, Zeb following closely behind. It was a little tricky getting him and the jar situated safely on the back of her bike, but Zeb tucked the jar inside his sweatshirt and held onto her with one hand while steadying the jar with his other. Luckily, they didn't have far to go. Still, she was relieved when they reached Raven's Crossing.

Zeb gave the tower room of his house a long look before heading around to the back. Someone had nailed plywood over the broken windows and tarped the damaged part of the roof to protect it from the rain. It didn't look much like a fairy tale now. It made Mariah sad to see the destruction

Kane had caused. The sooner they got him back in the cemetery the better.

Moose was waiting for them near the row of graves separating Raven's Crossing from the Hollows. With a low woof, the red-boned hound rose to greet them. His fur was wet, making his face look even darker than usual. He circled Zeb first, sniffing his jeans and shoes, and then did the same to Mariah. Then the dog sat down and cocked his head, as if waiting for a recap of their latest adventure.

"We caught ourselves a ghost, Moose," Zeb said, holding the jar up for the dog to see. The roiling smoke inside the jar looked like threatening storm clouds. Moose let out a low growl. Zeb bent over and tousled the hound's silky black ears. "Don't worry. As soon as we take care of Kane we'll all go celebrate. How do pancakes sound?" Moose's tail thumped happily. Zeb winked at Mariah. "Moose is in, how 'bout you?"

"I could do pancakes," she said. He looked so cute standing there she couldn't help but smile. "But only if I can have an equal amount of thimbleberry syrup."

Zeb grinned back at her. "I think that can be arranged."

And despite the coolness of the rain-kissed air, Mariah's cheeks warmed. She glanced past him to the seven headstones guarding the Hollows and her smile faded.

"Are those graves...?" She let her voice trail off, not sure how to ask the rest of the question.

"All the past Keepers," Zeb said.

Mariah remembered the names she'd read when she'd first seen the graves, and how they all had Zeb's last name. Raven. Then she remembered how the date on the last grave was so recent and new. Was that one Zeb's father? Her throat ached. To lose a parent was the hardest thing. She reached for Zeb's hand.

"I'm sorry about your dad," she whispered.

He looked over at her in surprise. His disarming eyes, one blue, one hazel, searched hers for a long moment. Then he squeezed her hand in return.

Moose barked twice, interrupting them.

She blushed as Zeb gently pulled his hand away. "We should probably go." He nodded his head in the direction of the Hollows.

"Keepers first," Mariah said, gesturing for him to lead the way. Because even though they had Kane trapped, she wasn't eager to return to his grave.

The path through the Hollows had been eerie enough during the day, but as twilight deepened into night it was downright scary. A cool breeze, like the brush of ghostly fingers, shivered across the back of her neck. And she hurried to keep up with Zeb. He didn't seem bothered by the darkness. But then he didn't keep tripping over the rocks and tree roots like she did either. Which was good considering he was the one holding the ghost jar. The shadows pressed suffocatingly close. And Mariah was almost relieved when they reached the cemetery clearing.

At least here she could see. Though the sight of all those warded graves made her shiver all over again.

"You still have the athame?" Zeb asked.

She pushed aside her leather jacket and unhooked the knife's fancy hilt from under her belt where she'd tucked it earlier. He nodded.

"Good. Keep it handy just in case."

She gripped the ebony handle of the ritual blade tightly. "Now what?"

Zeb lifted the jar. "We take this over there and ..."

Something loud hit the side of the glass, startling them. "What was that?"

The knocking came again, and this time Zeb nearly dropped the jar. He fumbled to hold onto it.

Mariah heard a low rumble. At first, she thought it was more thunder, but then she realized the vibrations were coming from within the jar. She watched in horror as first one crack appeared in the glass, then another. Right under Zeb's hands. She saw his eyes widen as he realized what was happening. Before he could carry the jar inside the protective wards of the cemetery gates, it jerked free of his hands and crashed to the ground. The glass splintered and the black smoke inside erupted loose. Zeb scrambled backwards.

"Run!"

Chapter Nineteen

Moose the Protector

An unseen force knocked Zeb onto the ground. Shards of glass pricked his palms and the air around him crackled. For a moment he couldn't catch his breath. Then he felt a weight on his chest, pushing him down. It got even harder to breathe. He struggled to sit up, but the invisible pressure only increased.

"Zeb!"

He could hear the alarm in Mariah's voice. She was in danger, too. Knowing he had to get her somewhere safe before Kane got to her, he clutched at the silver amulet around his throat. It flared hot, then cold at his touch. And the invisible force crushing him suddenly lifted. He gasped in relief.

Mariah rushed to his side, helping him to his feet. "Are you alright?"

"I think so," he said. But the words felt like a lie.

"What happened?" Her face was pale.

He looked down at the shattered ghost trap at his feet. "Kane broke out of the trap."

"How?"

Zeb could only shrug. He had no idea how the ghost had gotten loose, or what the source of his power was now that the girls' spirits were free. Kane was obviously a lot more powerful than he'd thought. Maybe that's why so many things in town kept dying. Maybe Kane knew how to draw energy from the living. It was a frightening thought. Zeb shook his head and glanced around the clearing. The cemetery, awash in deepening shadows, was quiet. But there was a growing vapor of darkness coalescing a few feet away from them. Kane. Zeb's blood ran cold as he sensed the ghost's growing wrath, because he knew it wasn't just directed at him.

He tugged at Mariah's arm. "You have to get out of here."

"Not without you," Mariah shot back with a stubborn shake of her head.

Knowing there was no time to argue, Zeb gripped her hand and ran. The woods enclosed them. All Zeb could hear was the thump of Mariah's boots on the hard-packed dirt path and his own ragged breathing. Broken tree branches snagged his sweatshirt and slapped his face. He kept running, not daring to look back. Finally, through the trees, he glimpsed the wide back lawn of Raven's Crossing, beckoning to him like a safe haven. His home had never looked so good.

He slowed to let Mariah pass him. "Go! I'll be right behind you."

Mariah tried to hand him the athame, but he shook his head. "You keep it; I've got this." And he held up his amulet.

Tree limbs snapped behind them and branches crashed to the ground, closer and closer. Kane was nearly upon them. Mariah turned and fled. Zeb watched until she was safely out of the Hollows, then turned to face the ghost's onslaught. His medallion started to glow. The thick darkness that was made of more than twilight and shadows loomed over him. He spread his arms out wide. Blocking the path, he braced for Kane's impact.

"Come on, Kane! Here I am."

But the ghost blew right over him. The powerful rush of swirling energy threw Zeb off balance. He stumbled and fell. Twisting around on the ground, he saw the black wave of shifting shadows emerge from the trees and head straight for Mariah. She was still running, but the ghostly tide of darkness was faster. Cursing, Zeb struggled to his feet. What did Kane want with Mariah? He was the Keeper. Why hadn't Kane come after him? Unless it had something to do with Mariah's resemblance to Mercy Gray. Or with the athame she was holding.

Heart pounding, he tried to run, but his body felt heavy, like he was stuck in a dream. Halfway across the lawn, the thick vapor gathered behind Mariah. Zeb watched in horror as a black tentacle detached itself from the seething mass. It stretched out and wrapped around Mariah's ankle, yanking her backwards. She went down hard. And for a moment Zeb couldn't see her at all. He yelled her name.

The cloud of darkness surrounding her started to morph, giving shape once more to Bartholomew Kane's twisted form. And in one of his clawed hands, he held the athame. Zeb saw the glint of light on the silver blade as Kane raised it high, the blade that stole souls, the one now aimed directly at Mariah.

"No!"

With a hoarse scream he fought to lift his feet, to sprint to her side, but it was like he was moving in slow motion. He watched helplessly as Mariah rolled onto her back and kicked at Kane. With a deep-throated growling laugh, the ghost shrugged off her attack. Then he swung the knife down. Mariah threw her body to the side, barely dodging the blade. Kane uttered an angry roar and lifted the athame again, poised to strike.

The sudden and deep baying of a hound sounded like a clarion. Zeb's heart leapt. From the edge of the yard, Moose charged across the lawn. His fur was limned with a fiery glow. The unflinching hound flew at Kane. For a moment dog and ghost merged into one, a melee of light and darkness. Then Moose burst through to the other side, landing atop Mariah right as Kane's athame swung down. The silver blade sunk deep into the hound's side.

There was a burst of brilliant light. Kane loosed a howl of pain as his ink-black shape began to shred. The cloud of darkness hovering above Mariah dissipated, but Zeb could sense that the ghost was not gone, only momentarily forced back. Then he saw Moose's body slump to the ground. And something inside him broke.

"Moose!"

The anguished cry tore from Zeb's throat. Freed from the invisible force that had been holding him, he sprinted across the lawn toward Mariah and the hound. Mariah's eyes were closed. She looked so pale he was afraid to touch her. But he had to know. With a trembling hand he hesitantly brushed his finger across her cheek. Her skin was still warm. And she was breathing. He leaned closer, checking her bared throat, but he couldn't see any knicks or cuts. Relief washed over him as he gently shook her shoulder.

"Mariah?"

She stirred but did not open her eyes. At least Kane's cursed athame hadn't touched her; he hadn't claimed her soul. All because of Moose. Tears sprang up in Zeb's eyes as he turned to check on his dog. The red-boned hound wasn't moving. Zeb pressed his face against the dog's dark head. Nothing. He ran his hand across the dog's still body. There was no visible wound, no sign of blood, but there was no warmth or life either. In saving Mariah, Moose had made the ultimate sacrifice. His loving, heroic, funny, faithful companion was gone. And Zeb lowered his head and let the tears flow.

CHAPTER TWENTY

RAZING KANE

KNOWING HE HAD NO time to grieve now, Zeb squared his shoulders and inhaled deeply, his breath ragged. He was fairly certain Mariah would come to on her own, that the energy from Kane's attack and Moose's rescue had only knocked her out temporarily. And Moose—he didn't dare think about Moose right now. The dog had saved her, he was certain of that. But oh, the cost.

He rose slowly to his feet. He didn't start this fight with Kane, but he would be the one to end it or die trying. Heat from the amulet warmed his skin through the fabric of his shirt. The protective energy was still there. The athame glinted on the grass. He picked it up, not wanting Kane to possess it again. Spidery cracks shot through the red stone in the handle. When Moose launched himself at Kane to protect Mariah, the blast of supernatural light hitting Kane's darkness must have shattered the stone. Kane wouldn't be able to use this knife for evil ever again. Zeb dropped it to the ground.

The ghost floated before him, more powerful and more corporeal than it had been moments ago. The dying flowers in town, the power outages, the broken branches and scattered leaves in the Hollows—Kane was drawing energy from everything around him. As Moose lay silent and still on the ground, Zeb wondered if Kane had taken energy from the dog, too.

Kane made a sound, a chilling imitation of laughter. "You are next."

Zeb had no idea what to do. Without salt or rue to make a circle, without a ghost trap, he wasn't sure how to fight this battle. He struggled to recall the things he'd been studying in the Keeper journals.

A ray of moonlight broke through the clouds and fell upon the Raven graves. Wet from the rain, they shimmered in the pale light. The Raven graves. Family. Blood. He could use that. It might work.

Zeb searched his pockets for anything sharp. He found his key ring and the small pocketknife he carried on it. Opening the knife, he ran the dull blade across his palm. He gasped as the tip of the blade penetrated his skin, and he pushed it deep enough to draw blood.

At the scent, Kane's ghost stood erect before him. "I could have done that for you." The voice was gravelly and deep.

Zeb shuddered. He gripped the amulet with his cut hand, letting the blood slip across the pendant.

"By the blood of the Keepers, Raven's blood, I banish you."

Kane cackled. "Keeper? You are hardly a Keeper. A child, maybe."

Kane's taunt slid off him like the rain. He no longer cared what the ghost thought. He was a Raven. From a long line of Keepers. This was his home. This was his fight.

He let go of the amulet and as it was exposed to the open air, the blood on it sang out. He couldn't logically explain it, this call, this reaching.

"I, Zeb Raven, Keeper of Grayhaven, banish you" His voice grew stronger, steadier.

The ghost faltered, and Zeb took a step toward him. Was it his imagination, or was light gathering above the Raven graves?

"Blood of Raven, I call on you to defeat the ghost of Bartholomew Kane and send him forever to the empty realm."

Empty realm? What was that? Zeb shook his head. Those words came from somewhere deep inside him, someplace in his core, a generational collective memory.

A glow rose from Mathias Raven's grave and formed into a ghostly figure, emanating light. The figure drifted over to stand near Zeb, and he heard it speak. "I, Mathias, blood of Raven, rise to banish you, Bartholomew Kane."

Kane's form wavered.

Zeb watched, astonished, as another light rose from the second grave and joined the first. "I, Thomas Mathias, blood of Raven, join to banish you."

Two more Keepers rose, Benjamin and Jebediah, the Raven brothers. They joined the others and repeated the same phrase.

Kane's smoky shape spun around, seeing the Raven ghosts behind him. He moved away from them, toward Zeb, who held out the blood-tinged medallion. The ghost let out a blood-curdling scream.

Nathaniel Raven joined the circle of light around the ghost, followed by Zebulon Thomas. A lump formed in Zeb's throat as he recognized his grandfather. Zeb's attention flicked away from Kane, and he stared at his father's grave, waiting. Would his dad appear?

Kane lunged forward, and a wave of paralyzing cold washed through Zeb, driving him to his knees. He fought to get up, but the chill was overwhelming.

A light rose from the last grave, drifted past Kane, and took form beside him. He felt a warm touch on his shoulder.

Dad's voice was quiet. "Get up."

"Dad?" he said, his voice thick. "You're here?"

"I never left you, son."

Zeb struggled to get to his feet, fighting through tears. As he rose to his full height, he realized the seven ghosts had formed a circle around Kane. Mathias was on his left, and his dad was on his right.

From the periphery of his vision, Zeb could see his father beside him. But more than that, he could feel his presence. Steady and sure. Zeb's eyes swept around the circle. Each of these men had filled the Keeper role before him. They recorded their experiences, leaving him a guide book as he took their place. And now they were here, when he needed them most, adding their strength to his, bound together by blood and by purpose. He turned to his dad who appeared healthy and strong as he had looked in his prime. Not thin and sickly like he'd been the last time Zeb saw him. All of the things he hadn't been able to say during Dad's illness welled up inside him.

"I love you, Dad."

"I love you, too," Dad said. He faced Kane in the center of the circle. "I, Thomas Benjamin Raven, complete the circle. We, the blood of Raven, banish you."

Zeb sensed the strands of power in the circle weaving together family, sacrifice, and dedication, until it formed an unbreakable rope encircling Kane.

"Now, son. Finish it," Dad said.

Zeb fought to keep his voice under control. "I, Zeb Raven, by the blood of Raven surrounding you, banish you from this realm now and forever!"

Energy surged through him, and a ring of blinding light surrounded Kane, growing to fill the circle and compressing the space around the ghost. The hands gripping Zeb's shoulders filled him with warmth and power, keeping the circle intact as the murky form fought against the light, lost shape, and swirled into a column of haze. A blast hit him, pushing him backward, but the hands on his shoulders steadied him. With a loud, thundering clap, Kane's ghost vanished, and the light from the circle dimmed.

Kane was gone, leaving a void of darkness that shriveled in on itself and disappeared.

It was over. Relief washed through Zeb like a wave.

His grandfather stood before him. "You are a fine Keeper, my boy. Grayhaven is in good hands."

"Thank you," Zeb said, pressing his hands together as if in prayer. "All of you." The Keepers nodded.

One by one, they faded out of his sight. Except his dad.

"Dad, I..." Zeb didn't even know where to begin. How could he express how much he missed him? How he hated the way he'd died? How alone he'd been? "I've failed. Being a Keeper, the business..."

The ghost of his father shook his head, and Zeb felt a warm embrace. "You banished a very powerful ghost today. You're a strong Keeper. I'm so proud of you and all you've done to keep things going."

Zeb clung to every moment, wishing his dad could stay. His father drifted off to the side and hovered near Mariah and Moose.

"Ah, Zigmund. My victorious protector."

The ghostly presence of Thomas Raven stroked the dog's head and placed a hand over the prone animal's heart. "It isn't time yet, old friend. He still needs you."

Moose whimpered and raised his head off the ground. Slowly, he rose to his feet. His tongue lolled as he limped over to Zeb and sat beside him, pressing his body against Zeb's leg.

Zeb dropped to his knees, all of his attention on the dog. His fingers trembled as he touched Moose's silken ears. The dog was warm. Real. Alive.

"I thought I'd lost you." Zeb's voice cracked. When he'd seen Moose on the ground like that, unmoving, the loss filled him with an emptiness he couldn't begin to face. He couldn't imagine a day without the cold nose that so often nudged him into action, or the wagging tail that thumped against his legs, reminding him that he wasn't alone. Moose was not only his friend, but the last living connection he had with his dad. Zeb sat on the cool ground and pulled Moose onto his lap.

He held the dog close and rocked gently, unaware of the crickets chirping, or the breeze ruffling his hair. He was only aware of Moose, of his warmth, of the comforting heartbeat steadying his own. "You're back. You came back."

It was over. Kane was gone. He and Mariah were alive because of Moose.

'Thank you for staying with me, pal," he said, pressing his face against the dog's body. "I can't do this without you."

Moose wagged his tail and, with a sigh, rested his head on Zeb's shoulder.

When Zeb finely raised his eyes, he saw Thomas Raven standing nearby.

"Take care of him," Thomas said. Moose wriggled out of Zeb's arms and sat before Thomas. Zeb rose to his feet.

"It's time you were free, son. Being a Keeper is enough of a burden. If you don't want the diner and the motel, let them go. Raven's Crossing, though...that will always be yours."

A lump formed in Zeb's throat. He'd thought for months now that he wanted to be rid of the diner and motel. Now he wasn't sure. But Raven's Crossing...that was where he belonged. He'd move back in as soon as possible.

Thomas Raven glanced over at Mariah. "She has no fear. That's an unusual trait. She was a big help to you through all of this."

"Yes, she was," Zeb said. To his relief, Mariah was stirring on the grass.

His father was fading. To have him disappear now would be like losing him all over again. "Don't go, Dad. I need you."

Thomas smiled. "I'm never far, son. You know that now."

As his father disappeared from sight, Zeb let his tears stream down his cheeks. Moose pushed his head under Zeb's hand and he stroked the dog's silky ears. Seeing Dad like that, healthy and strong, healed something deep inside him.

Zeb knelt and buried his face against Moose's neck. He hugged the dog. Kane was gone. Moose was back. And he was no longer alone.

Chapter Twenty-One

No Place Like Home

MARIAH WINCED AS SHE opened her eyes. Her head ached and the world around her was a blur of moonlight and shadow. Were those stars overhead or the aftereffects of Kane's attack? She blinked. Out of the corner of her left eye she glimpsed a strange flickering light. She lifted her head, squinting. Zeb?

He stood near the Keepers' seven graves. Two men were standing with him, but they didn't look quite right. There was an insubstantial quality to them that made her wonder for a moment if she was dreaming. Or hallucinating. Then the one on the left grew even fainter until he faded away altogether. And she suddenly knew. They were spirits. The one that remained looked remarkably like Zeb.

She heard the low murmur of Zeb's voice. Though she couldn't quite catch everything he was saying, one word came through: Dad. The ghostly figure had such a look of love on his face it was palpable. And Zeb. She'd never seen him so at peace. She watched as an aura of golden warmth encircled the two of them in its glow. That's what love looked like.

The sight of it generated a wave of longing inside Mariah so strong it lodged in her throat with a choking ache. She wanted that. Connection. Home. Family. To belong somewhere. To feel that kind of love in her own life. Her eyes blurred with tears, and she covered her face with her hands.

"Peace, Mariah." The words whispered in her mind and she felt a ghostly hand brush across her back. Rolling over, Mariah looked behind her but there was no sign of the ghost.

"Mercy?"

A faint shimmer of white on her right. A voice like a breath or a distant echo. "Thank you, Mariah Gray. And welcome home."

Mariah froze. Gray? Her last name was Moore. And home? What had Mercy meant? She searched the dark yard to ask but the ghost was gone. Sitting up, Mariah rubbed the tears from her eyes. She was alone once more, but the aching sadness in her chest had eased. Mercy's puzzling words had given her a fluttering hope. Could Grayhaven be her home?

A low woof interrupted her thoughts. A nose snuffled her knee and then the warm lick of a tongue kissed her hand. Moose. She turned. The hound cocked his head at her, as if asking if she was okay. She smiled and petted his silky ears. Then, leaning forward, she rested her forehead against his.

"Thank you for saving my life."

Moose woofed again and licked her cheek.

As she lifted her head, she saw Zeb standing over her. He looked tired but happy. Holding out his hand, he helped her to her feet. "You okay?" he asked.

She nodded, even though her entire body ached and her legs felt wobbly. But then she had been attacked by a ghost intent on killing her. Her gaze darted around the clearing.

"Is Kane...?"

"Gone," Zeb said. "Forever this time."

The wave of relief that washed over her was so strong it buckled her knees. Zeb quickly slipped an arm around her waist to steady her.

"You did it," she whispered.

"No, we did it."

He grinned down at her while Moose danced around them. The sudden intensity in his eyes filled her with unspeakable happiness. Standing on tiptoe, she impulsively wrapped her arms around his neck and hugged him. His arms tightened around her. She could feel his heart beating in time with hers as she breathed in the clean scent of his skin. It was a perfect moment. Then, with an insistent bark, Moose nuzzled his way between them, and they both laughed. Because he had done it, too.

THE LOW RASPY CAW of a crow greeted Mariah the next morning as she emerged from her motel room. Her bike was running well, but rather than speeding out of town like she normally would after a job, Mariah headed toward Raven's Crossing instead. Mercy's last words still echoed in her head and there was something she wanted to show Zeb.

The old Victorian's windows were gleaming in the late morning sunshine and the front door stood open, as if waiting for her. All traces of last night's storm were gone and the air felt fresh and cool. There was a familiar pickup truck parked in the drive with some boxes in the back; Zeb must have borrowed it from Carlos again. She parked next to it and removed her jacket and helmet.

Butterflies fluttered in her stomach as Zeb emerged from the house. He was dressed in blue jeans and a faded black t-shirt. His light brown hair was tousled and he was whistling. He looked happy. Warmth filled her at the sight of him and she waved in greeting. He grinned as he skipped down the porch steps and jogged over to where she stood. The haunted look was gone from his eyes.

"You're just in time to help me unload these," he said, gesturing at the boxes.

She frowned. "Is all this your stuff?"

"I've been staying at the motel," Zeb said, grabbing a box from the truck. "But it's time for me to move back home. I have a tower room to fix up and a cemetery to keep watch over."

A large crow flapped over their heads with a deep-throated caw. Mariah glanced up. It was the second time she'd seen it that morning. Did that make it one for sorrow? Or two for joy?

"That crow followed me here," she said. "You don't think it's trying to tell me something, do you?"

Zeb scanned the sky until he spotted the large black bird. "That's not a crow; it's a raven," he said. "And ravens are always good omens." He winked at her. She grinned back. She liked this version of him. Confident. And a bit mischievous.

Grabbing a small box from the truck, Mariah followed Zeb inside the house. She paused in the entry to look around. The only time she'd been inside the house was the day of the fire. To her surprise, there was no lingering smell of smoke. Except for the boarded-over windows of the tower room it was almost as if the fire had never happened. Another small proof that Kane hadn't won. And Mariah was glad that Zeb's home had not been destroyed.

"Zeb?" she called, not sure which way he'd gone.

"Up here," he said.

She followed the sound of his voice up the stairs to a large bedroom that overlooked the back lawn. A pile of clothes was strewn across the bed and Zeb was unpacking books into haphazard stacks on his desk. But Mariah was drawn to the window where she could see the Raven family graves standing like quiet sentinels at the edge of the woods. All the spirits there were at rest. She could feel it. She drew in a deep, cleansing breath, before turning back to the room where everything was a bit of a mess. But even that felt reassuringly normal. She set the box she'd carried down on the floor.

"I wanted to show you something," she said, pulling a wadded paper and some old photos from her pants pocket. She set the black-and-white photos on the end of the bed and smoothed out Fleur's sketch of a tree. She threw Zeb a nervous glance as he moved closer to peer over her shoulder. "This is Mercy's family tree," she said, tracing a finger over the names she'd filled in on the trunk and branches. "And mine." She pointed to the roots of the tree. "Here's Ezekial Gray." She moved her finger up the trunk to the branches. "His son, John. Then his grandson, another John, who married Matilda. To protect their child, they left Grayhaven and assumed her maiden name Moore. And you can follow this line all the way up to me. Mariah Moore."

Zeb's breath tickled her neck as he exhaled in wonder. "You're descended from John and Matilda Gray? That explains why Kane was so interested in you." He playfully nudged her shoulder with his. "And now here you are, back where you belong. It's like it was meant to be...Raven and Gray together again."

"Gray and Raven," Mariah corrected.

He laughed. "Graven?"

She groaned. "Don't ruin the moment, Zeb," she teased. But then she sobered. There was one last thing she needed to do. Reaching into the side pocket of her cargo pants, she pulled out Mercy's locket and opened it. One of the photos was smudged by a drop of rain, but the resemblance between Mercy and Mariah was clear. She brushed a finger across her ancestor's lovely face. Then reluctantly held it out to Zeb.

"Return this to the museum for me?"

He studied her face for a long moment, then took the locket. But he didn't put it in his pocket. Instead, he clasped it around her neck. "I think Mercy would want you to keep it," he said.

His hands straightened the chain, before coming to rest on her shoulders. When he didn't move away, she closed her eyes and leaned into him, reveling in his closeness and quiet strength. She had never felt this way before with anyone. Zeb's arms encircled her, and she listened to the steady beat of his heart. Something that felt a lot like joy unfolded in her own.

"I'm not sorry, you know," she murmured, raising her head to look up at him. "If I hadn't set Kane free, the souls of Aurora and the other girls would still be trapped with him."

Zeb cupped her cheek with his hand. His eyes, one blue, one hazel, held hers. "I'm not sorry either," he said. Then he gave her a conspiratorial smile. "I went into the Hollows and refreshed the wards this morning. Grayhaven should be quiet again. At least for awhile."

"Way to go, Zeb Raven," she said. "You'll be a great Keeper."

"And you?" he asked. "What will you do now?" His tone was casual, but she could feel his body tense as he waited for her answer. Did he want her to go? Or to stay? She wished she knew because she wasn't ready to leave. It was safe here with Zeb. And full of possibilities. Gray and Raven. She liked the sound of that. Maybe Grayhaven would end up being the home she'd always wanted. And Zeb? Maybe he was the one she'd been hoping for, too.

She drew in a shaky breath and stepped back. Her thumb touched the lotus blossom on the inside of her wrist for courage. "I actually thought I might stick around for a while, you know, in case you needed any help with anything."

"Anything, huh?" His voice was husky, and his eyes searched her face. "I like the sound of that."

She felt her cheeks grow hot, but she did not resist when he tugged at her belt loop. Pulling her closer, he murmured her name. She lifted her face to his. Then, his mouth mere centimeters from hers, he paused. And she saw the question in his eyes. In answer, she raised up on her toes and pressed her lips to his. Warmth like summer sunshine rushed through her as he kissed her back. It was their first kiss, but she knew it would not be their last. Because kissing Zeb was like coming home.

Moose bounded up the stairs, his tail whipping from side to side as he barged between them. He woofed at Zeb, then nudged Mariah's hand, asking for a scratch behind his ears. Mariah was relieved to see him looking so healthy and strong. She bent over and gave him a hug, laughing as his rough tongue tried to lick her face. She wasn't sure she wanted his kisses. But she didn't have the heart to push him away. Moose nuzzled her cheek, and she laughed again.

"What's that you say? You want some pancakes?" She threw Zeb a mischievous grin. "I think your dog is hungry. He keeps trying to eat me."

Moose barked and threw Zeb a hopeful look.

Zeb shook his head, but she could see the amusement in his eyes. "You can't be hungry, Moose. You just ate."

Whining, Moose tugged Zeb's shoelaces, pulling him toward the door. Zeb laughed and rubbed Moose's dark head. "Bottomless pit." Then he smiled at Mariah. "I suppose you want some pancakes, too?"

"I could eat," she admitted, loving the way that Zeb smiled at her.

"Come on then," he said, as Moose did a happy dance between them. He pulled his keys from his pocket and reached for her hand.

About the Authors

Amy Newbold and Lark Wright are sisters who brainstormed this story while on a trip to Devil's Tower. Since they share a love of family history and visiting cemeteries, it was only natural to include both in Ghosts of Grayhaven. Despite going on ghost tours and exploring cemeteries together, neither Lark nor Amy have seen a ghost...yet.

Connect with us! Stay up to date by joining Amy's monthly newsletter or by following Lark's blog.

Amy's Newsletter: https://subscribepage.io/FGApSB

Lark's Blog: https://larkwrites.blogspot.com/

Authors' Note

A shout out to Matt Newbold for his advice on Mariah's motorcycle. Thanks also to Daniel Newbold for being our first avid reader. Special thanks to artist extraordinaire, Greg Newbold, for the cover illustration, and to Val Paul Taylor for creating the cover design. We want to thank all of our family members who read and supported this project from the beginning.

For those who are curious, Moose is based on a Bavarian Mountain Scent Hound.

ALSO BY AMY NEWBOLD

Sweet & Clean Romance

Amidst Ruins and Remembrances (Victorians at the Beach series)

A Lady Most Alluring: A Grimm Regency Tale

Picture Books

If Picasso Painted a Snowman

If Da Vinci Painted a Dinosaur

If Monet Painted a Monster

For an updated list of Amy's books, please visit her website: https://www.amynewbold.com/